A LITTLE PIECE OF MIND

BY THE SAME AUTHOR

There's a Lion in My Bathroom
The Fearsome Beastie
Things You Never Knew about Dinosaurs
Princess Stay Awake
Little Bell and the Moon
Superchimp
Things You Never Knew about Santa Claus
Things You Never Knew about Dogs
Blank
One Hundred and Fifty-Two Days

A LITTLE PIECE OF MIND

GILES PALEY-PHILLIPS

unbound

First published in 2022

Unbound

Level 1, Devonshire House,
One Mayfair Place, London W1J 8AJ

www.unbound.com

Text design by Patty Rennie

A CIP record for this book is available
from the British Library

ISBN 978-1-80018-130-4 (hardback)
ISBN 978-1-80018-131-1 (ebook)

Printed in Great Britain by CPI Group (UK)

1 3 5 7 9 8 6 4 2

'A life is not important except in the impact it has on other lives'

JACKIE ROBINSON

IMPACT

Lying on the ground
with my head in my hands
and my eyes so heavy they close...
I try to prise them open.
They will be here soon
and they will ask questions,
lots of questions.
I lie on the ground,
silent, a smoking ruin beside me.
Crumpled metal strewn across
a street, now swarming
with the voyeurs of this carnage.

SOMETHING HAS HAPPENED

I hear whispers... and
voices;
voices and lights...
flashing lights, my eyes
struggling to focus,
everything around me going
in and out.
A bitter coldness takes
hold of me, like my veins are freezing within,
and I just want to sleep.
But something has happened.

WRITING STUFF DOWN

I'm trying to remember everything.
What I saw...
what I heard...
what I smelt...
My memories come and go...
        ... in waves.
When they come, they feel
painful.
When they fade, I feel
relief... freedom... clarity.
What I remember;
what I saw;
what I heard;
what I smelt.
All I remember is her
right now.
I need to write
it down...

BEFORE

My name's Hobs.
Short for Hobart.
I was named after the place
of my conception.
Hobart is the capital city of
Tasmania, the Australian island state.
I've never been there, but my parents
visited once.
I was born on
the south coast, near the sea.
The birth was hard...
My dad told me
that the midwives had to use
forceps to get me out and my
mum thought they were salad tongs
and shouted at them to keep
the kitchenware away from her.
She never saw the funny side
when he mentioned them.
Like she'd lost her sense of humour
when she had me.
Still, I knew my dad loved me
even if he didn't always know quite
how to show it.

LIGHTHEADED

Steam starts filling the room and
the water is hot and flooding the bath.
The heat makes me feel faint,
lightheaded… giddy.
I sit on the edge of the bath and my mind soothes.
I settle into the bath, the mottled
tiles dripping with condensation,
my thoughts dripping away
into the water
and I feel no pain
and I stare ahead at the taps.
Drip,
drip,
and I'm back being a child again,
maybe three or four, playing
with some cheap plastic toy.
Drip,
drip,
dripping
and I return to now.

MY BRAIN ADJUSTING

'Hobs...'
I startle awake, thinking I heard
someone calling my name, just once
from downstairs, not sure if it's real
or a dream. It felt
so vivid, a voice I recognise,
but as I start to feel more
awake, my brain adjusts to
it being a dream, not real,
just my subconscious
in light sleep.
When you don't sleep well, light sleep
is all you can aim for
and I'm thinking about
everything, like there's fifty tabs
open on a browser.
These moments come and go.

DAD WAS A GIANT

It was the morning
and I was awake.
I hadn't slept well for two years,
not since she left,
since Mum…
left us.
When she met someone else
and decided
to move away.
With insomnia you're neither
asleep nor awake;
somewhere in between.
Dad was still asleep,
snoring, snorting.
Working nights meant
we crossed paths,
passing shadows,
but never
really spent time together.
Dad worked in the local
hospital, nursing.
I'm not sure I've ever helped anyone
in my life. Dad did it every night.
My dad's a big man: big hands,
big feet, everything a little out of
proportion. Whenever he's asleep
various limbs stick out from under the duvet,

like he's a grown-up
sleeping in a kid's bed.
When I was little, I told people
my dad was a giant, like the one
in 'Jack and the Beanstalk'.
Kids would never believe me till
they saw him.
He's nothing like a giant, though.
He's quiet,
unassuming.
He'd never make a fuss
or get angry.

ONE DAY MERGING WITH ANOTHER

I got my bag ready,
trying to picture what lessons
I had, one day merging
with another.
Maybe it was English
or art – I forget.
I took the entire stack
of books by the side
of my bed, just in case.
I now looked and felt like
a packhorse, as if I was about
to go on an expedition. My
shoulders hung heavy, and
my posture paid the price.
Dad peered out of his room
and smirked at me as I tried to
coax the bag onto my back.
'You look like that game, Buckaroo,' he said.
I snorted a laugh
and nodded as he retreated
back into his room.
'I'll be down in a bit,' he said.

MIKE BILK

I'd put the TV on
and some guy...
... some politician was
spouting something about God
and power and helping people.
I didn't relate to
something about them
and us, but I'd started listening
too late.
He was some guy running
for office.
His name was Mike...
Mike Bilk, handsome, well groomed
and slick, he sounded well rehearsed.
He talked about a higher power,
about his beliefs and how
they'd make him suitable to govern, because
a god had said so, like he was better than
other people.
The interviewer started in again.
'So, what do you say to the rumours
you were heavily involved in the
cover up of the Circano deal?'
Mike Bilk just smirked, and
you almost knew what he was
going to say: whatever it is
has nothing to do with him.

'I can't listen any more,' Dad said.

'He speaks like a guy who doesn't play fair.'

Then he turned it off.

REMNANT OF LOVE

I thought Dad was going to pick
up his guitar
from the stand in the living room, but
he just brushed past it.
Our home was always filled with
music when I was younger, but
he hardly played any more.
She'd taken everything from him,
his ex-wife,
my mum.
He used to play in a band – that's
how they met – so the memories
of that were there
in our living room; the guitar
a remnant of love
and loss.
The memories continued to linger around me,
then follow me
out of the door.

COLLEGE

College was a fifteen-minute walk
for me.
I walked at a pace which was
not slow...
but... slowish.
Either side of me along the road
there was no nature, just deserted buildings,
remnants of a high street once
humming with shoppers.
I stopped by in town, and grabbed a
coffee. It was so cold out
and the coffee
felt so good in my hands.
The clouds grew moody
in the sky, which summed
this place up.
People feeling low; nothing to
do around here.
We lived in a dead town; you could
kind of understand why a guy
like Mike Bilk would resonate.
It looked like it
might rain or even snow, it was that cold.
I sipped tentatively at the coffee
as the hot steam kissed my lips,
as it seeped through the hole
in the lid.

I eased it off and the steam
now covered my face
and the warmth felt good.
I ripped open another
brown sugar and poured
it in. I wanted this to taste really sweet,
take the edge off the bitter
double espresso.

IT'S OUR THING

I saw Jonas by the gate.
'How's it going, man?'
he said.
'I'm alive,' I said.
'What's with the bag, dude?' he said.
'You moving out? Jesus, man,
what have you got in there?'
'Couldn't remember what I was doing today,' I said.
'So you brought everything?' he said.
'Yep, I brought everything,' I said.
Jonas was taller than me, but
he hunched his shoulders so much
that when I talked to him, it always
felt like I was talking down.
He'd always be in the same clothes: khaki
shorts with DM boots, and his hair
looked like it had not been washed
in months. He'd got a whole early nineties
look going on, grungy, like the music
he listened to... the music I was into: Pearl Jam,
Soundgarden, Rage Against the Machine, stuff
people don't really listen to so much these days.
But it was our thing.
But I didn't look like Jonas, I just
looked regular: skinny jeans,
trainers and white tees with logos on,
as little effort as possible.

CATALOGUE GIRL

We walked through the reception area
to the common rooms.
There was a girl by the pool table
talking to Mia
and Tam. They were wearing almost
identical outfits:
long tees and black leggings
with black running trainers.
They looked like they were
heading for the gym, if it
weren't for the heavy make-up
and branded bags.
I heard Mia huff.
'Sigh!' she said.
I wondered how we'd got to
a stage in our evolution
when someone had to actually
say the word 'sigh' rather
than just expressing it physically.
The other girl looked at me.
She smiled.
I tried to smile back
but I'm not sure I did.
She looked amazing, not like people you'd
see in real life, or here, for that matter.
More like
from a catalogue or a movie.

She turned back to Mia
and Jonas picked his nose, while
he fiddled with his hair.

JENNI

'Her name's Jenni,'
Jonas told me.
She'd recently moved
back to the area
but she was new to our college.
I strolled over and placed
some coins on the table.
I was next to play.
The winner kept the cash
that had built up
on the side of the table.
I'd watched her play, and she was
good; I couldn't keep my
eyes off her, watching her
stroke the cue, potting
ball after ball, cleaning up.
Our eyes met several times
as I'd purposely stood
too close to the table, so
she had to ask me
to move,
my eyes moving from hers
to her lips and back again.
It wasn't long till she'd won, and
it was my turn.
I knew I could beat her
and I needed the pot.

The coins were high,
balanced by the pocket.
'You want to break?' she said.
'Sure,' I said,
trying not to sound
too confident.
I broke and didn't sink a thing;
not one ball dropped, and
she was straight on the cue ball.
'Tough break,' she said,
before giving me a wink.
She started potting stripes, then another
and another
and another.
She was cleaning up
before I could even get back
to the table.

SEVEN-BALL RULE

She scooped up the coins
and dropped them in her bag.
'Are we playing seven-ball rules?' she said.
'What's that?' I asked.
'If you don't pot anything, you
have to drop your trousers,' she said,
looking me straight in the eye.
'I've never heard of that,' I said.
'Let me get you a Coke or something.'
'OK, thanks,' I said,
and we headed to the vending machine.

BACK TO NOW

I'm standing in my room
and it feels airless, and
I'm finding it hard to breathe.
I almost feel like I don't remember
coming here, as if I've woken
in this moment...
... having skipped a section.
I can still smell her
on my skin,
on my hands.
I keep thinking why...
why was she there?
And my head starts to hurt,
then my eyes and face.
And all I want is
to close my eyes and sleep.
I hear my dad's voice say, 'It's going to be OK,'
and, 'Don't worry' – the sort of things
he thinks I want to hear.
But I know he's scared
and he knows I'm scared.

PEACE AND QUIET

Dad runs me another bath.
There's still some blood
on me…
he says.
And I sit on the bed.
I need some peace;
peace and quiet.
I don't want to think,
not for a while.
I just want to be.

HEAD IN HIS HANDS

I hear Dad in the bathroom
and through a crack in the door
I can just about make him out.
He's sitting on the edge
of the bath. The enamel is chipped and worn
and the grout surrounding the tiles
that line the walls is stained with
flecks of mildew; it clearly hasn't
been cleaned properly in a while.
His face looks pale as he puts
his head in his hands
while I'm thinking back.

ENGLISH LESSONS

Turned out we had English together,
just a row apart.
Mr Playdon started talking about the
week's assignments – and the groans.
I looked over at Jenni
and she was rolling her eyes
and pretending to yawn.
I smiled and she giggled.
For the rest of the lesson
I couldn't stop looking over
at her.

TWISTING THE STRAW

I saw Jenni across the food hall.
She gestured to me
to come over,
come over and talk.
'Hey, you!' she said.
'What are you doing this weekend?'
I told her I hadn't quite figured it out,
but we both knew we wanted
to see each other.
She was sipping on a smoothie,
while twisting the straw;
it was a bright orange colour.
'Does that stuff glow in the dark?' I asked.
'It's mango,' she said,
'and passion fruit, I think.'
'It looks disgusting,' I said.
She laughed.
'Yeah, it really is,' she said
as she pushed it away.
'Can I get you something else?' I asked.
'Sure, thanks – can I get a Diet Coke?'
I grabbed us two cans
and I sat back down opposite her,
wondering what to say next,
but I didn't feel I had to,
it just felt OK to not say
much at all, and

Jenni seemed to feel the same.
We just sat, watching
everybody else.
'I love to people-watch,' she said.
'Make up little stories in
my head.'
'Did you make up a story
about me?' I asked.
'Of course,' she said.
'So, what was it?' I asked.
'I can't tell you.
That would spoil it.'

MAKING PLANS

I watched her as she
drifted away…
We made a plan
to meet up…
She looked back once.
Our plan was to meet
at lunchtime, for a coffee.
She looked
back
over her right shoulder.
Just one look
over her right shoulder,
smiling, a white-teeth smile.
Coffee together, our plan.
Smiling her white-teeth smile.

THINKING OF HER

They say no one is truly dead,
not if they have experienced love.
I'm not sure if I have, but I know
I have never been closer than with her,
with Jenni.
I'm looking at Dad through
the crack in the door
and I'm thinking of her.

HELPING WITH LEAFLETS

Jonas was looking at his phone,
then he put the screen up to my face.
'Look at this douchebag!'
On the screen was Mike Bilk,
his face staring back at me,
his eyes looking into my eyes.
'This guy is running for office, and
he wants to hike tuition. This guy,
all the things he says
about minorities and women too.
I mean, look at this guy.
Man, he makes me sick. What a prick.'
I looked at Mike Bilk staring back at me.
He had a striking lantern jaw,
the lower part projecting out,
sinking his cheeks in.
I didn't think
I'd ever heard Jonas talk about
anything other than video games
and TV shows.
'That Jenni, she knows him,' he said.
'Jenni?'
'Yeah, man, straight up knows that guy.
I think she's helping with leaflets
and such,' he said.
'Maybe he's OK?' I said.
'Yeah, maybe. You must really like her,' he said.

MY MIND IS A MAZE

The bath is run and I sink in.
My mind is
a maze, of thoughts, of emotions.
Dad helps to wash off the blood
from my hands,
from my arms, nursing me.
And even with him here
I feel more alone than ever.

SWITCHING CHANNELS

My mind keeps sparking,
like my brain keeps
switching channels
now...
then...
here... there.
I wish I could switch off;
closing my eyes only makes it worse.
The next thing I know,
Dad is dragging me out
of the bath, shouting my name.
And I'm in between being
awake and asleep.

COFFEE SHOP

Jenni and I met
at the mall
by the coffee shop.
She wanted coffee –
a latte. Franchise coffee,
franchise milk,
franchise steam.
We sat in a corner on a sofa,
sitting towards one another,
our legs touching; it felt good.
It felt right, comfortable.
I watched how her lips moved
when she talked; the curves
were perfect and defined.
We talked for so long, we noticed
the barista looking over,
wondering if we were ever going to
order another coffee or a franchise snack.
We'd outstayed our one-coffee welcome.
But we ignored him and we laughed about
him staring at us, huffing when other customers
couldn't find a seat.

We talked about why she'd come
to this town, how she and her
mum were starting over.
How her dad was gone, but

I didn't like to ask how.
'He was a lot older than my mum,' she said.
'I do miss him,' she said.
I wondered if he'd died or just left.
She didn't say, and she looked
upset, so I didn't probe her further.
Then she asked about my parents.
I told her that they must have been in love
at some point, but after me it sort
of faded away, for my mum at least.
'They do say it's better to have loved once
than to never love at all,' she said.
I smiled.
'When I see how she made my dad feel,
how it made him grieve so,
I'm not so sure,' I said.
'I could never do that to someone,' I said.
She smiled at me,
a full smile, like I'd said the right thing.

BLOTCHED WITH BLOOD

I'm lying on the floor.
As the water runs away
the blood leaves a ring around
the bath, a little red legacy
of something that has
happened
before.
Dad is hurrying around, picking up
towels, now blotched with blood
that's rapidly drying.
There's panic in
his face.
I keep saying, 'It's OK, Dad,
calm down,' but he
doesn't seem to hear me.

HOPING FOR SLEEP

Dad puts me into bed
and I feel like a small child.
He sits on the floor
with his back to the bed, not saying
anything, but him being there is a comfort.
And I close my eyes, in the hope
that sleep might come.
When I wake he's gone
and the clock says 3.36 a.m.
I throw off the covers and
sit up, my mind racing.
I feel giddy, and I wonder if I sat up too fast.
Then I remember what she said
when I last saw her.
But I didn't think anything of it
at the time.
And it still doesn't make sense
to me.

WE MET WHEN WE COULD

We met whenever we could.
Breaks, after class, after college,
whenever we could.
The way she talked, the smoothness
in her voice. She had this way about her
I'd never experienced before: it was
hypnotic;
it was beautiful.

DAY AFTER DAY

She was in my thoughts
and I was in hers, I knew that.
She put notes in my bag, in my pockets,
in my hands.
Secret notes, secret messages.
Her feelings,
her thoughts,
and not just surface stuff,
not just the 'I Heart YOU'
kind of thing.
It felt real.
So I knew,
I was in her thoughts
as much as she was in mine.
And she texted me photos,
loads of selfies,
each with a different expression
and different look.
One with a smile,
one with a grin,
another with a grimace.
Others she had her tongue sticking out.
It was her face
day after day…
… with words,
her words… just for me,
and lots of emojis,

little laughing faces with tears
of joy, high fives and fist bumps
and my favourite of all – a little smiling poo!
All to show she was thinking of me.

VOTE FOR MIKE

I was walking home
and on every post and signpost
was Mike Bilk's face.
VOTE FOR MIKE!
on the newspaper stands,
in people's front windows.
VOTE FOR MIKE!
I saw one with a Hitler moustache
drawn on with permanent felt-tip.
One said,
VOTE FOR DICK!
One said, ASYLUM SEEKERS ARE WELCOME.
I saw a van go by and the guy
in the passenger seat threw
a milkshake out of the window
straight at a billboard,
straight into Mike Bilk's face.
The thick sticky white drink slowly ran
down his chin, like it was dribbling
out of his mouth, like a flaccid penis
leaking ejaculate.
This one said,
VOTE FOR MIKE! *If you're racist*
and the face had devil horns coming out of it.

A DIFFERENT LIFE

Waiting for sleep
so I can start a new day.
Something new,
something different.
Maybe a different life.

FIRST-WORLD PROBLEMS

I was back at home and
I was sitting on my bed
when I heard a tap at my door.
'Are you in there?' she called.
I opened the door
and it was Jenni.
She shuffled in and I sat back down.
She straddled me.
'Your dad said I could come up,' she said,
and I placed my head on her chest,
and she was so warm,
it felt like home.
'Good day?' she said.
'Some of it.'
'What parts weren't?' she asked.
'Oh, just little things. I forgot
my password for student login
and then Wi-Fi went down.'
'Wow,' she said.
'You had it hard! First-world problems,
Hobs, first-world problems,
like having to stand on public
transport or being cold-called,' she said.
'Or dunking a biscuit in your tea
and half of it falling in?' I replied.
'Exactly,' she laughed.
'It's blighting this world!'

I laughed and she tried to
tickle me.

STAYING IN THE MOMENT

Our eyes met and
our warm lips embraced.
It was a delicate touch.
My hand slid down her back
as hers went lightly to
the back of my neck, where
her fingers spread through
my hair, and it made me
tingle.
I'd never been in this situation
before…
Never kissed a girl like this
before…
My feelings for Jenni were strong,
even though we hardly knew
one another. I was lost in those
thoughts when I should have been
staying in that moment.

NOT NOW

'Can't we stay right here?' I asked.
'Like this?'
'Not now.'
She was pulling her jeans back up
and buttoning them slowly.
'I've got to go,' she said.
'I'm helping with the campaign and
promoting his new stronger borders policy.'
'What campaign?' I asked.
'Mike's, of course.'
'Mike? Why are you working with
that guy?' I asked.
'He didn't seem like a good guy,
when I saw him on TV.'
'He's been good to us, Mum
and me. I feel I kind of
owe him.'
'Owe him?' I asked.
'Yeah,' she shrugged.
'He helped us out getting
a place when we moved here.
He knew my dad, they were friends.
He's done so much for us
since Dad. There was this deal—' She suddenly broke off.
'... And it went bad.
I've gotten to know him – he's
not like people think.

He's nice…
he's kind. He was the only one
who came to help us when Dad…'
It felt like she was a little
agitated, like she wasn't sure she
should be saying this.
'I'm sorry if I said the wrong thing,' I said.
I smiled and decided to change
the subject.
'Will you stay for some food?' I asked.
'You should meet my dad.'
'I just did,' she said.
'You should meet him properly, I mean.
I'd really like you to,' I said.

PLEASE STAY

I heard Dad calling for dinner.
'Please stay?' I asked.
I must have looked kind of desperate, as
she almost looked sorry for me.
'I'll stay,' she said,
'but just for a bit. I can
probably be a little bit late.
But only because it's you!'
We headed downstairs.
I just wanted to hold her
again, just for a moment...
just me and her.
So I stopped her halfway down; she was
on the step above me,
her blonde hair draped
over my head, like a blanket
keeping me warm,
and I wrapped my arms firmly
around her back and she groaned
in a nice way.
I could've died right there.
It was perfect.

MIRRORED

We were in the kitchen sitting opposite each other.
Dad was serving us spaghetti.
'Do you like to cook, Mr Vallens?
This looks amazing,' she said.
'Please, call me Frank,' he said.
'Well, I wouldn't say I'm any good, but ever
since it's been just the two of us, I've
tried to cook all types of stuff.'
She looked at me, and smiled.
A gentle smile,
a reassuring smile.
I looked at Dad, whose smile somehow
mirrored Jenni's.
'It's good to meet you, Jenni,' Dad said.
'You too.'
'I see you have a guitar – do you play?' she said
to both of us.
Dad looked surprised, almost embarrassed.
'I used to,' he said.
I looked over at Jenni and subtly shook my
head, and I could see
she understood me:
Don't go there.
'My dad used to play too,' she said,
'before he killed himself.'
Dad and I looked at each other
a little stunned.

'I'm so sorry,' Dad said.

'Me too,' I said hurriedly.

'I'm not sure why I said that –
I've never really said it out loud
like that before,' she said.

'It's OK,' said Dad.

'Sometimes the moment just seems right.'

'Yes, you can say what you like here. We're
here for you if you need us,' I said.

Dad smiled at me, then Jenni
smiled back.

'This is great spaghetti, Frank.'

'Thank you.
You can definitely come again.'

And we all smiled.

THE SURFACE PEOPLE

Dad was in the kitchen, sorting out
the plates in the sink.
'I'm going to make like a tree,' she said.
I looked at her, puzzled.
'And leave... silly!
I'm so late!' she said,
before patting me on the head
like a puppy.
I smiled.
'That's terrible,' I said.
'When will you be finished?'
'Ah, these campaign meetings go on.
It'll be a late one.
I'll catch you later in the week.'
'Later in the week?' I asked.
'Why not tomorrow?'
'I've got so much on,' she said.
She crouched down so her head
was facing my midriff, her hands
placed gently on each of my thighs.
'You understand, right?' she said.
'I've got lots of things going on right now,
but I really like you...
and I will make time... I promise...
soon.'

I tried to form a smile,
but I don't think she could see it.

CAN'T WAIT ANY MORE

I didn't see her or
receive a text from her
for days,
so I started to hang around
after her classes.
It was one afternoon
The bell was about to go.
and I couldn't wait any more.
The shrill of the bell
made my heart jump
and I felt excitement
as I finally saw her face.
As she walked through the door.
'Where have you been?' I asked.
She just smiled coyly.
'I've just been busy with
the campaign. I got permission to
take a few days off classes.
You understand, don't you?' She said this
gently placing her hand on my chest.
Just her touch made
me feel special.
'You're not mad with me, are
you?' she asked.
'No, not really. Just be nice
if you could have messaged me.'
'I promise I will – it won't

happen again. Now, where's
my kiss?'
She grabbed a fistful of
my top and yanked
me towards her and our
lips locked like magnets.

HER ALONE

We walked back to mine and
we hovered around outside the front door.
I saw Dad in the kitchen
preparing an early supper.
'Do you want to come in?' I said.
But she just smiled and shook
her head.
'I better not.
I got chores to do at home before
my mum gets back.'
We kissed and I held her face
in my hands, gently stroking
her cheeks, and her skin was
so soft, without blemishes
of any kind.
Neither one of us wanting to be the first
to break away.
And then I'm inside and heading
to my room, still thinking about her
and her alone.

DEEPER AND DEEPER

My eyes feel drained, sore to touch
and blood-red to look at.
My brain hurts, thoughts
foraging deeper and deeper
and taking hold.
I want answers; I need
answers. But what is the puzzle?
And I just want Jenni.
I sleep from time to time,
hours passing, and I hear the traffic
moving up and down.
I grit my teeth and sit up,
heading to the living room.
I switch on the TV
and the screen flickers before appearing,
but it's the usual
late-night infomercials
about life insurance and new
operating systems.
I'm in between now, neither awake
nor asleep. Trying to think of anything
but Jenni.
My eyes flick open
and I momentarily wonder
where I am.
The TV is still buzzing.
Then his face is across the screen.

DIFFERENT

A few days later, Jenni had promised
to call me after college.
I was at home and it was late,
but she was haunting every one of my thoughts.
The door went, and Dad answered it.
'Hobart, it's Jenni
for you,' he shouted.
He always seemed to call me by my full name
when something was up.
I trundled down the stairs to see her, and
he gave me a disapproving look
before he turned away towards the kitchen.
Jenni was standing in the doorway,
but she looked different, didn't seem
herself.
'Hey you,' she slurred before she stumbled
into me. She'd been drinking.
I could smell it on her.
'What's up?' I said,
but before she could answer,
she'd started to slump to the floor,
her eyes closing as she mumbled
something about her mum.
I managed to get her to my room
before she fully passed out.
I shouted out for Dad, but he
didn't hear me at first, but by the third

time I'd shouted, he'd appeared
and was helping me get her up on my
bed. He checked her over.
'Calm down, Hobs,' he said,
seeing me look agitated.
'She's fine. Maybe not used to
drinking too much before.
Let her rest.' He pulled a blanket
up from the bottom
of the bed and placed it over
Jenni's legs.
He propped her top half
up against the headboard.
'If she looks like she's
going to be sick,
shout for me,' he said.
I felt Dad's hand on my shoulder
trying to give me reassurance.
'I'll get some water,' he muttered
as he left the room.
It was several hours
before she woke.

RISING AND FALLING

I sat by the side of the bed,
watching as she slept.
My eyes fixed on her chest,
focusing on each breath
in and out...
... in and out.
Rising and falling
... rising and falling.
But there was no other movement,
and she looked different somehow,
maybe older.
Little creases began to
appear on her face where
it was pressing on the bed.
As my eyelids started to feel
heavy, I forced
them back up. I didn't want
to miss this moment
of just me and
her.

HESITATING ON A WORD

She couldn't remember much
when she eventually came round.
'What happened?' I asked.
'Oh, it's nothing really.'
'Nothing? You were so drunk!' I said.
'I know, I got out of hand. My mum and I
just got into an argument about my
dad,' she said.
I wondered what she was thinking.
She looked like she wanted
to talk, hesitating. I wasn't
sure what to do, whether
I should probe, or wait
for her to tell me.
'He was never depressed – at least
I don't remember him being,' she said suddenly.
She straightened her back
like she felt emboldened,
as if a weight was lifting.
'My mum and I,' she said,
'we never talk about it.
I was about fifteen. He just left,
walked out of the house, and that was
the last time I saw him.'
I thought how awful that must have been.
'Where did he go?' I asked.
'It was a few days before

they found him. He'd driven to
the coast and thrown himself off
a cliff.'
I looked at her now, and she didn't
seem upset; she was composed.
'I'm so sorry, Jenni,' I said.
'I've never really told anyone before.'
And she took my hand in hers.
It felt special that she was able to
tell me
her secrets.
'What was it that made him, you know...?' I asked.
'We found out a few weeks later that he'd
lost all our money – he'd been doing
lots of business deals. One went really bad.'
'So why did you and your mum argue?'
'She just gets protective sometimes.
Thinks I haven't been home enough,
what with the campaign
and us.'
'Us?' I asked.
'Is there an us?'
'Of course, silly.'
She let go of my hand and
put it on her head.
'My head is pounding,' she said.
I got her some tiger balm
and a wet flannel.
I looked her in the eyes
and for the first time

in my life
I wanted to look after someone.

IS THIS WHAT LOVE IS?

I just looked at her.
Her face,
her hair,
her hands
holding my hands.
Is this what love is? I thought.
Caring so much about someone
you hardly even know.
I fished out my phone from my bag
and fumbled about with my headphones;
the cable had become all twisted.
'Why does that always happen?
I coiled them up perfectly,' I said.
'First-world problems,' she mumbled groggily
and we both smiled.
I placed one headphone in my ear
then the other in Jenni's.
I pressed shuffle on my playlist
and we just lay there, listening,
not saying a word.

HEADING HOME

We must have drifted off,
when all of a sudden, her phone
bleeped and
Jenni sat up to look at it.
'I need to get home,' she said.
'My mum will expect me home.'
'I'll walk you home.'
'No!' she said. 'It's OK.'
And I wanted to insist,
but I could tell she wouldn't
change her mind.
This was a different her.
She scrambled a kiss and was gone.
As the door shut,
I found myself pacing the room,
the floorboards creaking,
before I stopped myself.
What was so urgent?
Was she in trouble? Maybe
she needed my help.
I decided to follow her,
just to make sure she got home
OK.
She wasn't how she usually was.
I opened the bedroom door and
headed down the hall. I grabbed
my jacket and ran out of the house.

FOLLOWING

The cold air hit me in the face
and I could feel my eyes
start to water...
and drip.
Across the street two kids
were kicking a ball to each
other, unaware
of me,
of Jenni, who I saw heading
north, towards town,
towards the centre
of this little place
where we lived.
I put my hood up.
A car suddenly pulled out
of a driveway
and I ducked down behind a bush
to the side of the house.
As I looked up
I saw her.
I hoped she was OK.

TWITCH

A blue car, the windows
blacked out,
and Jenni had her head
right up to the window,
almost inside.
I crouched down and all I saw
was her feet, and they twitched
like she was nervous.
I could see her toes
curled inside her open-toed shoes
and then I saw her feet
go from one side of the car
to the other.
The passenger door opened
and I saw her feet
go inside
and by the time I stood up
the car was gone.

HOPING FOR SLEEP

I'm back sitting on my bed
and a hard-edged light
flicks into the room,
through a small gap
in the curtains, then it
crawls along the floor up to my face.
It's morning. And I hear
the front door open and slam
closed. It's Dad, back from work.
I lie back on the bed,
hoping for sleep.
Dad drifts past my door
and his head eases into my room.
'Can you hear me?' he whispers.
But I've got my eyes closed now
and I pretend I haven't heard.

LICENCE PLATE

I couldn't make out
the licence plate, but
the car was a metallic blue,
kinda sporty, like it had been
worked on, a project,
souped up.
And it moved away quickly,
the tyres leaving little
marks as it burned off.
And I asked myself,
Who?

EIGHT DIGITS

The average person can hold
up to eight digits in their memory
at any one time.
Eight digits.
I just need to remember.
I'm an average person.
I have an average memory.
I must remember.

EMOJIS

The next time I heard from Jenni
was a couple of days later.
She sent me
a message:
a text, an emoji of a
coffee cup, with
a tag that said 2 p.m.
I was just by the entrance
to the food hall, when I saw
Tam and Mia near the doorway.
They didn't see me, but I heard my name,
so I moved in closer,
but not so close that they'd
know I was there.
'What does she see in him?' Mia said.
From the corner of my eye
I could just make out
Tam, who was leaning up against
one of the tables.
'I don't get her,' Tam replied.
I wanted to walk in,
show them my face,
show them I knew what
they'd been saying, but I didn't.
I couldn't. It wouldn't have been fair
to Jenni – they were
her friends.

So I made a hasty retreat.
We met
and she kissed me on the cheek;
it felt so good.
'I came after you the other night,' I said.
'Whose car was that you got in?'
'Are you stalking me now?' she giggled.
'No, I was gonna catch you up,
make sure you got home OK.'
'It was Mike, Mike Bilk. Look,
he's OK. He's harmless.'
Harmless?
What's harmless? A small animal?
A squirrel? A mouse?
'So he just took you straight home?'
'Are you getting a little jealous, Hobs?' she teased.
'No, just asking.'
'He's OK,' she said.
'He really looked after us,
especially after what happened
with my dad.
The Bilks are OK, Hobs.
We had dinner with them recently. My mum
came too. Really, you can trust them,' she said.
'Even Stefan.'
'Stefan?' I asked.
'Tam's new boyfriend
Stefan? He seems like a bit of a douche.'
'No, he's OK. Look, they're not like a
normal family. Mike's a powerful guy,

and his wife's a little messed up,
probably drinks too much, but they're
no more fucked up than any other
families I know.' She said this
to put me in my place,
which she had.

BACK ON THE BED

I sit up, slowly leaning my ear
towards the door, and then I
collapse back onto the bed.
I must have been asleep for ages.
Staring up at the ceiling, I notice
a mark on the woodchip.
I lift myself up onto my knees
trying to focus on the mark,
my left eye closed,
my right eye fixed.
This little mark, above my bed.
I can feel myself edging closer
and closer and my hand reaching up
till the tip of my index finger is right
below it
and the mark drops
onto my finger
and another appears
in its place, and it's wet
and it's red.
It looks like blood.
I wake up.
On my bed.
My phone buzzes
but I ignore it.
Looking up, the mark on the ceiling is gone.
Downstairs I can hear the TV is still buzzing.

I head down, wondering
how long I've been asleep.
Dad's bedroom door is open
and he's not there – must have left
for work. Have I been asleep all day?
The TV is showing a shopping channel, and
a guy on the screen
is selling rotisserie kits.
The room is really dark now.
The guy on the screen is now selling
Tupperware and I look away,
and when I gaze back
the guy on the screen is selling
lampshade cleaner.
My phone buzzes again. It's
a message, but I can't be bothered
to look
and now the guy on the screen is selling
butt plugs, in various colours.
I wander into the kitchen
and open up the fridge.
The light doesn't work
and I can barely see inside.
I feel around, until
my hand caresses the milk
and I remove the cap and
glug straight from the carton.
On the screen the guy is selling
insurance with cover for accidents
that happen in the bedroom.

My phone buzzes again, and this time
I pick it up
and it's a missed call
and it's from Jenni's phone.

LINE IS DEAD

I look at the phone again
and dial back.
The line is dead.
I restart the phone
and recheck the calls list
but I can't see her number any more.
It's gone.
I stare at the phone.
It's sitting face up
on the coffee table.
The screen is black now,
on stand-by,
in reclusion...
napping... waiting there,
like me, for the next
pulse... indication... bleep
of life.
Waiting for something.

NOTHING

A few days later I was in English class,
thinking about Jenni,
and she wasn't there.
What was she up to?
My mind returned to the lesson.
Thinking about Jenni
and she wasn't there.
We were reading a poem
and the last words on the page
read 'sexual glue'.
Giggles rang out around the room.
I kept checking my phone.
But nothing.
I flicked a note to Tam. She was
sitting adjacent to me,
not really listening, just looking
at her phone, using it as a mirror
while she reapplied her lipstick.
It just said,
'Where is she?'
I saw her scribble
from behind her book,
then she waited, checked
no one was watching,
and flicked it back.
The note landed in my lap.
I opened it, trying to be discreet.

And all that was written was a
question mark.
I could feel my heart thumping.
Where the hell?
It had been days.

UNDER THE DOOR

My head started to
jettison sweat.
Was Jenni in trouble?
Something felt very wrong.
And I headed
straight to the nearest bathroom.
There was one guy inside.
He looked up from the urinal,
then shook himself off
and did up his zipper.
He looked at me
and I realised I was staring,
so turned and went into the
nearest cubicle.
Soon as the door was locked
and just as I sat down,
a folded piece of paper
slid under the door.

A CLICHÉ

Stefan Bilk,
six-two, tanned and trim.
A cliché.
Not dumb, but not clever.
But very popular,
so very popular.
I could see what girls saw in him.
Having a dad as a local politician
gave him a kind of authority,
like he was better than
others.
His mum stayed at home – you never saw her much –
and that's all I had on him, really,
that was as much as I knew.
Oh, and it seems he'd fucked most
of the girls in our year.
And, by the looks of it,
Jenni too!

POOL ROOMS

Jonas waited
outside the pool rooms,
slipping what looked like
bits of paper
to kids who sidled up to him.
As dealers go, he wasn't
very inconspicuous, but I doubted
he cared.
We gave each other a nod
as I wandered past, not wanting
to cramp him...
... disturb him...
ruin his space...
Inside, the room was filling out,
people playing pool... laughing.
Music flooded the room,
bashing my ears...
... thumping,
and I walked from table to table,
looking,
seeing,
hearing,
breathing heavily.
Outside, the light from a lamp post
struck the pavement
in front of me.
I leaned against a wall,

blew out my cheeks,
pulling in my breath,
putting off
what I was going to do,
putting off
what I might find out.
But I knew what I had to do
and I opened up the piece
of paper again,
the picture of Stefan
and Jenni.
Together.
Holding each other.
I tapped up the table
back inside,
nearest the entrance.
I would get the next frame.
I would play the winner
between Micky G
and Stefan Bilk.
Micky G was a big guy, worked
out a lot, a bit of a roid head,
so you never knew what mood
you'd find him in.
I wanted Stefan to win.
I needed Stefan to win.
I had to get to him,
a chance to talk
one on one,
me and him.

INSIDE

The paper was heavy
in my pocket,
like a lead weight.
My phone
vibrated, but I ignored it as
Stefan Bilk went for a
cut to the middle pocket,
but the black went in off the
blue spot, and it was
the first time he'd lost that night.
Micky G berated
him about it as
Stefan headed to the bathroom.
I followed him, adrenaline pumping.
Once we were through the door
I slammed him up against
the wall;
his slick black hair,
gelled tight
like tarmac, didn't move
one bit.
My fist met his face
with such force
that I felt like I'd struck
the wall behind him.
Blood gushed from his nose.
Then suddenly Tam was stood in front of me

screaming at me
to stop.

LIGHTHEADED

The thoughts make me queasy
and I start feeling
a little lightheaded, my eyes flickering
as if someone has set off a strobe light.
And then I'm focused again.

AGAINST THE LINES

'What the fuck, man?' he shouted.
'What is your problem? Do you know
who my father is?'
'Are you seeing Jenni?' I asked.
'Jenni? Is that what this is about?
Jenni?' He began to laugh.
'Sure, we went together once,
but she's not my type. Too needy.'
I threw another punch, but
this time it struck his throat
just below his chin. I felt his
Adam's apple push back towards
his spine.
He started to cough violently.

FACES

I awoke just as light was creeping
out from behind the blinds.
Five fifty-one a.m.,
I looked at the clock.
The picture just
to the side of it.
The light from the clock glowed
against their faces.

SITTING HERE IN THIS MOMENT

It must have been
a couple of days after
the pool rooms.
Still nothing from Jenni.
Why did I care about this girl so much?
I was lying on the field at college,
staring at the sunlight,
thinking about Jenni.
I was all alone
with my thoughts.
Then I saw a face above
mine: it was Tam.
'Hey you,' she said.
'Thought I'd come and sit with you.'
And we just sat there,
me and Tam,
not really talking,
just staring at the sunlight
together,
sitting there in that moment.
'I know why you went mad
at Stef,' she said.
'I was the one who
put the picture under the door.'
'You?' I said.
'I was just so mad at Jenni.
I thought you'd just get mad at her,

not get in a fight with Stefan!'
'I can't believe you, Tam –
what were you thinking?'
'I wasn't. Look, I've spoken
to Jenni about it.'
'You've spoken to Jenni?' I said.
'Yeah, just on the phone, it's cool.
We're all cool.'
'What do you mean we're all
cool? I'm not cool.'
Tam gently placed her hand
on my shoulder.
'It's all just a misunderstanding,
by me,' she said.
'A misunderstanding?'
'Yeah. Stef had a row with his folks.
He couldn't get hold of me and
he happened to see Jenni – she
was just there. It was just a hug.'
'So, who gave you a photo?' I asked.
'Oh, it was Mia, she was coming out
of her gym. She's just looking
out for me, Hobs.'
'Or stirring shit up?' I asked.
'It's not like that,' she replied.
'Well, what is it like then, Tam?'
I shrugged off her hand
from my shoulder and
stood up abruptly and walked
away.

'Come on, Hobs. It's all
OK. Chill.'
Tam's voice faded into the distance
as I spied Jenni at the far end
of the field.
About to head out of the entrance.

NOTHING GUY

The streets were busy.
Jenni hadn't returned
any of my calls
or texts.
I wondered if she knew
about me fighting with
Stefan. She must have done.
Maybe it was Stefan's car
she got into?
Nothing felt quite right.
I started to think maybe
something was going on with Jenni
and Stefan.
My mind started racing
with thoughts, jealous thoughts.
It made sense for her to be with
someone like Stefan, not someone
like me, a nothing guy.
I just wanted to talk to her.
Tell her I'm an idiot
for getting angry.
On the way home
police officers and security
trucks were pulling up in the town.
The next day there was the rally.
Scaffolding was being erected
and banners were being strapped

between street lights.
The next day
Mike Bilk was going to be talking...
running for office, with his
wife and son by
his side.

HEART POUNDING

It rings again.
The vibration in my hand
is violent, like an electric shock,
and the light emanating from
the screen is so bright
I have to look away.
The pattern of the screen
still stings each time I blink.
I just about manage to
touch the screen to answer
and as I lift it to my ear,
I'm confronted by
a high-pitched beeping sound.
It goes right through me
and it feels like my heartbeat
is pounding in time with it.

PICK IT UP

I wake up to find a bowl
of warm milky porridge by
the side of my bed,
by the side of my clock,
and next to that is a flyer
for the rally, with a note
written on it from Dad
to pick up milk.
I pick it up.
As I do, a spark
in my head jolts
me forward and something
comes to mind.

THE POPULIST

Every local news channel,
every radio station in the area
was talking about Mike Bilk
and his views
on the local economy, on health,
on the environment,
on the people, on immigration.
His views,
his populist views, not being
challenged, going mainstream.
Fuelled by a horde of acolytes and
social media ad campaigns, and
on every local news channel,
on every local radio station,
a movement seemed to be growing
behind this man
to give him power in
this area, to be elected and have influence
on government.
But I kept hearing some people bring up
'JUSTICE FOR CIRCANO'.
Questions from interviewers,
and chants from crowds.

TIPTOE

I see Dad asleep as I tiptoe
past his room.
In the bathroom everything
is neatly laid out, my toothbrush
next to the sink, the handle caked
in paste, dried and crusty.
I fill up the bowl with cold water
and plunge my face straight into it
and under the water.
I open my eyes and the
water stings.
Now I'm truly awake, just
as the phone in my pocket
starts to vibrate.

NO SIGN OF JENNI

I checked my watch
as the lunch bell was
about to ring, and
still no sign of Jenni.
I waited in line,
picking up items of food
and arranging them
on my tray in a neat little
line.
Carton of milk,
tub of yoghurt,
packet of crisps,
cheese and pickle salad sandwich,
all in a line.
I paid at the counter,
and behind,
by the double doors, I saw Jenni.
Jenni and I sat in the food hall
and she shared my lunch,
my sandwich,
my salt-and-vinegar crisps.
The sandwich had been sitting in a warm place,
as the lettuce inside had become
limp and flaccid. I started picking it out
then placing it back in the empty
plastic case the sandwich came in.
'Where have you been?' I asked.

'What do you mean?'
'In class today, and the last couple of days,
you never showed up!'
'I'm so sorry, I just couldn't face it.'
I tried to follow her eyes,
but they darted around,
looking left and then right,
not landing on anything for too long,
before coming back to mine,
where they finally landed
and locked.
Jenni got up and walked
over to Mia
and Tam.
Mia was short, with straight
blonde hair. Her nose was pierced, which
by the standards of the Surface People
made her edgy.
College is made up of
Tams and Stefans…
… the Surface People.
That's what Jonas and I called them.
People trying so hard
to be whatever
the others expected,
never truly being themselves. Most
of them would probably
end up like their own parents,
slogging it out in the rat race while
clinging to their loveless marriages.

I didn't relate to any of them:
Tam,
Stefan,
Mia, Rita…
these people I knew
but not really my friends.
They talked; she giggled,
looking back at me;
she smiled.
I was happy.
Was she happy?
The way she looked at me,
it lifted me and I thought
she must be.
'Will I see you later?' I asked,
as she sauntered over.
'You might,' she said.
'But you know? I still got to do
my own thing, too.'
'Your own thing?' I asked.
'Yeah, you know. Look, I like you.
I like you a lot, but I got
loads going on right now,
what with the campaign and assignments
and finding my way around here,' she said,
holding my hand, like she was
comforting me.
'Do you want me to back off,
is that it?' I asked.
I could feel my hands were

becoming clammy, and my
heart was beating faster.
I didn't want this to end.
'No, of course not,' she said.
I felt my heart start to ease
down again.
'It's just a really complicated time,
and I need to make time for everything,
but I promise you're high up the list.'
She squeezed my hand as a way
of reassuring me.

LEFT TO RIGHT, RIGHT TO LEFT

We said goodbye at the entrance
to the food hall.
She said she'd call me
just as soon as she got home.
People walked past us
left to right,
right to left,
a dual carriageway of students.
And we kissed, tasting each other,
and it felt so good.
And our hands stroked as we parted.

It's cold and
through the window of my room
I see the snow melting,
becoming slushy
and dirty on the road outside.
Just looking at it
sends a shiver meandering
down my spine.
I'm arranging my things:
my desk, my lamps, turning my bed
to face north,
when a new memory laps like a wave on
the shore of my mind.
Another fresh ripple
of what went before.

FOLLOW

This was the second time I'd followed her.
This time I watched her heading into
Mike Bilk's campaign building. The
office appeared to be shut down
for the day: no lights on, just
a smattering of vehicles in the
car park.
What was she up to?
I hung around for ages, but
I didn't see her come out.
After a while I decided to head home.
See if she might call,
like she said she would.

TALK TO YOU

It was 11 p.m. when she finally called.
'Hey you,' she said,
'what's up?'
'I wanted to see you,' I said,
'talk to you. I think we need
to talk.'
'OK, babe.'
She didn't sound like her.
'Have you been drinking?' I asked.
'Maybe a little,' she said.
'Just a little bit, tiny
little bit of drinky for me.'
She started to giggle.
'Shall I come over?' I asked.
'Ha, yeah, my mum would
love that,' she said.
'When will I see you?' I said.
She paused for what seemed like
ages.
'Meet me tomorrow, at the rally.'
'At the rally?' I asked.
'Why there?'
'I need to go, Hobs.
Pleeeeease, I know
the Bilks; I've been helping Mike
with the campaign.'
'I would do anything for you,' I said.

'Would you?

Would you really do anything for me?' she asked.

'Anything.'

'That's good to know,' she said.

Then the line went dead.

WRONG TEAM

Jonas called me.
'We're meeting in the square,' he said.
'For what?'
'We're protesting, dude,
against Bilk,' he said.
'There's loads of us going down.'
'What time are you getting there?
I'm meeting Jenni.'
'Jenni?' he said.
'You're picking the wrong team, man!'
'What do you mean?'
'You'll figure it out, man.'
And the line went dead.

TIP... TAP...

I tap the answer button
and put the phone to
my ear.
And the line is quiet.
I tentatively speak.
'Hello.'
But nothing,
then tip tap,
tip... tap... tip... tap,
the sound of dripping water...
rain... or a tap.
Tip... tap... tip.
Then the beeping starts again,
getting louder
and louder.
Then nothing,
and as I look up,
in the bathroom
mirror is a face
and it's not mine.

DOESN'T PLAY FAIR

I didn't get to the rally till around noon.
Crowds were scattered around.
It wasn't a huge turnout.
There was a couple with T-shirts
emblazoned with the face
of Mike Bilk.
Vote Mike.
Vote for Mike Bilk.
Good old Mike Bilk, the guy
who stood for something; the guy
who my dad said didn't play fair.
There seemed as many people here
in protest as well as
support.

RIGHT-HAND SIDE

It's Jenni's face that's staring back at me,
unwavering, eyes glued to mine.
On her head, to the right-hand side,
is a wound
and a trickle of blood
is running down the side
of her face. I step back
in horror and before I know it
only my face remains
staring back in the mirror.
Suddenly I sit upright.
I'm in bed,
sweating… not sure
what day or what time
it is any more,
and my mind is back
at the rally.

WAVES AND SMILES

Something wasn't quite right.
I saw her
across the street;
she waved and smiled
but it
evaporated quickly.
I suddenly felt like this thing we had
was slipping away.
My lips started to quiver, and I couldn't tell
if it was because I was cold
or just anxious.
I just wanted to hold her,
touch her hair
and lips
and face,
breathe deeply
into her ear and tell
her I was there for her; whatever
it was, I'd make it go away.
In this moment, I'd
release the chains;
I'd summon the hounds
to ravage whatever it was
that was making her
feel this way,
with her now-evaporating smile.

LISTLESS

Am I going mad?
Why am I seeing these things?
Seeing her
on my phone,
in the mirror.
Was she a ghost, the figure?
The apparition following me?
I feel haunted…
… everything seems
darker right now, as if someone
has adjusted the contrast
on the world.
Then and now.
After
and before.

ONE, TWO, ONE, TWO

I ambled over,
looking at my feet
as I walked.
One in front of the other.
Keeping count.
One, two.
One, two.
I moved my head up
and she was right in front of me.
Looking back at me
but not at me.
She was trying to act normal
but it was making her act strange.
I could see Jonas and a bunch of others
over in the square – they had made
placards, all shapes and sizes.
Pictures of Mike Bilk
with words I couldn't quite make out
spray-painted across them.
They'd made a real effort.
The smattering of people listening
paid them little attention.
I was not even sure they were
gonna make much of an impact.
No one here really seemed engaged, apart
from the hardcore Bilk fans,
who were near the front.

Jonas waved and ushered me over.
But I tried to be subtle
as I shook my head.
I think Jenni knew
but she didn't say anything.
She was just staring away now,
staring at everything, yet
staring at nothing, vacant.
Nervous.

WHERE IS THE GIRL?

'Are you here?' I asked.
'Yeah, sorry,' she said.
'Just tired.'
'I'm not surprised,' I said.
'You seemed wasted when you called.'
'When I called?'
'Yeah, you called me last night!' I said.
'I don't think so.'
'You definitely did!
You told me to meet you here.'
'And here you are,' she said.
'But I don't remember,
I'm sorry.
Things are a little confusing right now, Hobs.
I'll tell you sometime,
I will.'
I went to touch her hand,
to hold it, but she turned away.
'I need some water,'
and she wandered over to the store.
What was with her?
Where was the girl
who'd wrapped herself around me
in my room?
She had held me.
The girl who I thought
had feelings for me.

This was not her —
this was someone else.
Someone I didn't recognise,
someone I didn't know.

MY THOUGHTS

My thoughts are sparking, fully functioning,
making everything around
appear like someone pressed
the mute button, like white noise
in the background,
and I know I need
more answers…
but what questions
do I ask myself?

GHOSTLIKE

As she came out of the shop,
sipping from a bottle of water,
purified,
still water,
she hesitated
and looked ghostlike.
Just then the announcer said,
'Put your hands together for
the one and only Mike Bilk.'
And we strolled over to listen.

LONG DAY

Will it be a long day?
Can I jump off?
Can I bail out?
Find some perspective,
find some relief from all
these questions.

SMILE

I went to hold her hand
but she brushed my hand away.
She turned and smiled at me.
I think she was trying to reassure.
Her smile said,
Not now, not here.
You can read so much in a smile.

TAKING HIS TIME

Mike Bilk was on a stand
surrounded by a couple of hundred
people, maybe not as many as
he'd have liked…
… he'd have wanted.
The mic was in his hand
and he was taking his time
to start, to begin.
The pause was long, and
I could see the beads of sweat
on his head and I followed one
as it wriggled down the side
of his face, before plopping
on his shirt collar, soaking in.
And then he began.

SPEECHES

'I'm standing here today
as your chosen candidate.'
A voice rang out from the crowd,
just behind where Jonas
was standing.
'What about Circano?
You were involved, right?'
The crowd lay silent, then
an eruption of jeering.
The security and police started
to move across to where
Jonas and the others were now
shouting,
'Crooked Bilk, crooked Bilk,'
in a steady rhythm.
A guy in a suit clambered onto
the stage, flapping his hands
to quieten them down.
'Stop now, stop now. Mr Bilk
has been on record regarding this
matter.
If you have any serious questions, you
can ask them at the end, like everybody else.'
He stepped aside gingerly, avoiding a
bunch of wires on the ground.
Mike Bilk stepped back up.
And continued.

The crowd lapped up his words now, his
smiles and his promises. He was into
his rhythm.
Mike Bilk was untouchable right then.
This was his moment.
He was silk, suave and irresistible
right then, in that moment.
The crowd applauded at the right time
and booed and hissed when he mentioned
his opponents. This was his
political pantomime: he was both
the hero and
the villain.
And Jenni was beside me.
Shoulder to shoulder
we stood, and she now reached
out for my hand, and I could feel
her nails digging into
my palm.
I could hear Jonas
and his troop – they
jeered and waved their placards,
seemingly making very little effect, until
one girl struck a flare
and some police
and security surrounded them.
And they were filtered away.
One by
one.
I saw Jonas, and he was shouting

something at the top of his voice,
something I couldn't quite make out.
I stepped back against
a lamp post.
Leaning up against it, my eyes
felt heavy and I could have slept
right there, in that place.
A smattering of applause,
and a few whoops and cheers
slowly faded away and tailed off
at the end of Mike Bilk's
speech. No one seemed to have heard
Jonas shouting.
Jenni looked kind of upset.
'You OK?' I said.
'Sure,
just tired.'
I went to kiss her
and she let go of my hand
and turned her head
so I missed her lips,
to be met by her cheek,
where I landed my kiss, not
where I had intended.
But contacted nonetheless, something
we hadn't had much of
recently.
Moving off, I followed the
line of her eyes,
and she was staring over

at the Bilks,
at Mike,
at his wife, Andrea,
and Stefan.
She was staring at Stefan Bilk.
Behind her head I saw a post
with a flyer stuck to it,
with the head of Mike Bilk
and 'Vote for Change…
Vote for Mike',
covered with what looked like
permanent pen and the word
'Twat'.

SIGNS OF MADNESS

I look again at the flyer
by the side of my bed.
I pick it up,
trying to focus on it.
On the corner of it, something
is stuck.
The corner of something else.
Another flyer,
maybe a poster pasted next to it
when I ripped this down –
I did rip this down, didn't I?
I find myself talking out loud.
My dad used to say that talking
out loud to yourself was the first
sign of madness.
I think I'm beyond madness now.
Talking to myself is a regular
occurrence right now.
This thing on the corner – why
does it seem so significant?
And then it hits me.

HIS MOMENT

Mike shook hands
with people as he swam
through the crowd.
Some patted him on the back;
others hugged him.
His crowd.
His moment.
And trailing behind
were Andrea
and Stefan.
They'd come by us.
Jenni.
Me.
I looked at Stefan.
He didn't look back.
I hung back, but Jenni stayed there.
Mike shook her hand.
'Hello, Jenni, thanks for coming today,' he went.
'Thanks for all your help.'
Then Jenni and Stefan exchanged
knowing glances.

HEADACHE

I'm thinking of these things
and my head hurts inside
and out.
The more I remember,
the more intense
and uncomfortable it becomes.
I try lying down on my
bed and closing my eyes
a while, but there is
no reprieve.

LOOKING AT MY FEET

'What did he mean, "help"?' I asked.
'Oh, nothing much.
Just gave out some leaflets,
put some posters up,' she said.
'Let's get out of here, Hobs,'
and she pulled on my hand. I followed
like a lost puppy dog.
I looked at my feet as we walked
and my shoes looked so old;
worn-out old, but good old,
like they were meant to be that way
all along,
that they must have looked so wrong
when they were new.
I felt a little worn, not
so new. Maybe I looked better
a little worn.
Jenni looked new, but good new.
I wondered if we looked strange together, if
we were on different levels: her new
and me worn.
Maybe she liked worn?

EACH OTHER

We walked through the park
and stopped by the swings.
I sat on one and Jenni
sat on the other.
We swung in tandem,
not saying anything,
just enjoying each other's
presence.
At least,
I thought so.

A LITTLE STRANGE

Life could be good
if we stayed in this moment.
Life could be good in the
here and now.
Jenni and I
and no one else.
Life could be great.
I think we were meant to be
together; she made me feel
like we were.
I looked over at Jenni
and she seemed upset.
'What's up?'
'I don't know,' she said.
'Things are a little strange.'
'Do you want to talk about it?' I asked,
but she shook her head.
I wanted to talk to her about
the picture, her
and Stefan Bilk, but it didn't seem
the right moment.
'Can you just hold me?' she said,
and she came over and sat
on my lap.
I wrapped my arms around her,
a blanket of skin and bones.
I kissed her forehead

and kissed her cheek,
and a tear rested on my lip – I
could taste the salt.
Holding her tight and not knowing
what to say...
... what to ask.
Later I just watched her step onto a bus
and she was
gone.

FLYER

I'm thumbing the flyer
as I lie with eyes
tight shut, on my bed.
The weathered flyer
and some of it is coming away,
but most of it must be still stuck…
stuck to the lamp post.
Most of Mike Bilk's face
is still stuck to the lamp post;
most of 'Vote for Change'
and 'Vote for Mike'
is still stuck to the lamp post
and most of the word 'twat',
written in permanent pen.
Stuck next to it is
a poster; it reads 'Waterside Scandal'.
I start to rethink that day,
and the rally,
and Jenni,
and the last moments
we spent together.
Memories looping again…
and… again.

INQUIRY

Circano was a set of apartments.
Buildings developed by a property company
called Night Hunter Holdings.
Reading on, I learn that
Mike Bilk was a major shareholder
and oversaw a lot of the big
decisions, one being the use
of cheap materials on many aspects
of the buildings.
There was a huge fire during
construction; several workers died
and several more were injured.
A huge inquiry followed –
lawsuits, scandal.
Everyone lost out, except Bilk.
Mike Bilk came away clean.
Only Mike Bilk;
the only one. This is why people
were talking, why people
thought something stank.

FOR THIS LONG

It had never been for this long. It seemed
different this time. The
way she was had bothered me.
I hoped she hadn't gotten
herself in trouble.
I was worried. Really worried.
I saw Jonas by the bike racks.
I asked him when he last saw her,
when he last saw Jenni.
'I don't know, man.
Like, the day of the rally,
after she was with you.'
Had she got off the bus?
But I saw her get on,
saw it drive away.
'Who was she with?'
'Just Mia and Rita,' he said.
'Oh, and that guy, Stefan.'
Why was she with Stefan?
I didn't say anything more
and Jonas seemed distracted,
so I walked away...
I saw Stefan
by his car
and he was with Tam.
I walked over and Stefan
started to move away

but I grabbed his arm.
'Stay,' I said.
I looked at Tam
and she flicked her auburn hair
off to one side, and I noticed
her eyes narrowing.
'When did you last see her, Tam?'
But she didn't say anything;
her eyes just flickered left
towards Stefan, who
hung his head.
And I couldn't tell if she was
just lying or giving out a signal.
Stefan's demeanour
was different too, like he knew
something, like he felt guilty,
my gut
telling me I may have got this wrong.
Then, maybe, my gut just had shit
for brains.
'I'm not sure I know
what you're talking about,' Tam said.
'Jenni,' I said.
'I haven't heard from her.
Message me if you see her.'
And I turned and walked away
and I didn't look back, and
she was shouting something.
I couldn't make it out.

STATEMENT

Jenni was officially missing.
It had been over a week now.
No one had heard from her.
Her mum was beside herself.
That day she would be making
a statement
in front of cameras
for the media.
Holding a picture.
A picture of Jenni,
her face,
the face of the girl
I love.
Her mum looked
utterly worn out, large
bags under her darkened red eyes.
She looked as if she might break down
at any second. The intensity
of this moment was making
that a distinct possibility.

LIGHTS, CAMERA, ACTION

Lights…
'I ask that anyone who has any
information
on Jenni… my Jenni.'
Camera…
'I really just… want to see
my Jenni… again.'
Action.
'If you see this, Jenni…
please come home, get in touch,
let us know you're OK.
Please, Jenni,
please.'
Cut.
'We'll need to do that again,'
said a guy standing by the camera,
staring down at
Jenni's mum.
'Is that OK?
Really emphasise the "my", OK?' he said.
'Before we get everyone else in.'
I thought Jenni's mum
might be about to break.
Lights…
'I ask that anyone who has any
information
on my Jenni.'

Camera…
'I really just… want to see
my Jenni… again.'
Action.
'If you see this, Jenni…
please come home, get in touch,
let me know you're OK.
Please, Jenni,
please.'
Cut.
'That's much better,' said the man again.
I'd really like to have hit that guy
right then.
I stood in the background
behind the cameras,
the photographers and journalists,
the police.
I was just another onlooker…
… but I wasn't…
I was part of Jenni's life
and she was part of mine,
and I wish I'd said those
words,
those three little words.
While I had the chance.

THEY WANT TO SEE ME

They called around midday.
They woke up Dad.
They want to see me,
have a little chat, the police,
about what happened,
about Jenni,
about me.
Dad says he'll come,
take a night off.
I'm glad he'll be there.

QUESTIONS

I'm sitting at a desk.
The room is bare, apart from
a few chairs and the air-
conditioning unit in the corner.
'Do you have any idea where she might be?' he asks,
trying to sound authoritative
but calm.
I just shake my head
and turn my lip up.
Just then the door opens:
a lady, about thirty-five years old,
tall, wearing a tight suit, which
looks like it's been cut wrong.
'This is Detective Sergeant Bellucci –
she is assisting me on this inquiry.'
The guy asking the questions,
his name is Cole; he's kinda scruffy,
shirt hanging out one side of his trousers;
he looks like he hasn't slept;
unshaven,
unkempt.
'You realise this is routine?' she explains.
'We're just trying to establish all the facts,
make it clear in our minds.'
'Well, she had dropped off the radar before,
just for a few days. I thought
it might just be her needing space

or something,' I say.

'We know, Hobart, that Jenni got picked up
by' – Bellucci looks at a sheet beside her
on the table –
'a Stefan Bilk, probably
the night of the rally.'

Stefan Bilk? Why was she with him?
'How do you know that?' I ask.

'Stefan told us,' she says,
like she's hoping for a response.

I'd thought it could be Stefan,
but I didn't know who
or what to believe any more.

'Where did he take her?' I ask.

Bellucci leans forward on her folded arms.
'He mentioned that they drove around
for a while and then he took her home.
Jenni's mum has corroborated his story: she
saw his car pull up outside their house.'

'But I saw her get on a bus.'

'I guess it's possible she arranged to meet
Stefan without telling you. Is it
possible that Jenni and Stefan are seeing each other
behind your back?' As she says this
my head begins to throb, as if her words
are my thoughts, attacking me.

'Yes, it's possible,' I say.

'Now if there is anything else you can think of?'
My mind is so busy, I'm finding it hard
to retrieve it all. 'OK, thank you, Hobart,

we really appreciate
your time. We realise this
must be a very
difficult situation for you,' Cole says.
I can't help but think
this guy has done this before,
like he has
a routine response.
As soon as I get outside
my head begins to hurt even more
and I feel unsteady on my feet.

PROTECTOR

Dad meets me outside the police station,
where he'd been waiting for me.
I didn't want him to come in.
I thought it would upset him.
It's funny how, as we get older,
our roles start to change.
Protector becomes
protected.
I want to keep Dad away from
this; he doesn't need more worry.
I want to do this on my own.
Find Jenni on my own, and
it's not fair on Dad.
He doesn't say anything,
he just puts his arm around me
and holds me firmly, like
he's trying to squeeze some reassurance
into me.
He looks tired. A busy night shift.
So many frantic nights: the city never
stops, people getting hurt and ill
twenty-four seven, and it's taking its toll
on Dad. But he never says anything
and he never complains.

EVERY PAIR OF EYES

We walk along the road, and I feel
every face I see, every pair of eyes
watching, looking.
We stop at Uncle Bernie's Burgers.
I order a cheese and bacon
and Dad just has fries and a tea.
We sit in the window,
in a booth,
across from one another,
not really talking.
Dad reaches for my hand,
then the food comes out.
And the moment is gone.
I'm glad he's taken the night off.

NEED TO THINK

Back at home, I go straight to
my room,
desperate for sleep, my eyes
so heavy, so painful.
I paw my way along
the mattress, dragging
the covers across
the floor behind me, then
over the top of me,
my head hitting the pillow
but my eyes
staying wide
open.
The more trouble you have with sleep,
the more it starts to invade your thoughts,
your life,
everything.
But maybe today I should stay awake;
today I need to think,
to work stuff out.
To find out the truth,
to know the truth.
My thoughts are racing again,
like they are clashing with
one another, and it hurts my head.
The pain drifts from one side of
my forehead to the other.

It is searing and my eyes
feel blurred, and I start to rub
my head violently, try to
rub away the pain, and as quick
as it came, it fades and there is
a moment of
clarity.

STOMACH TURNS

I got home and Dad
had left a note.
It read,
'Jenni's mum called.
She'd like to see you.'
My stomach turned.
I hadn't seen Jenni,
not since
she went missing.
I'd never met her mum.
I wasn't sure she even
knew much about me...
about us...
Jenni and me.

SUBURBIA

Jenni's mum lived in
a quiet suburban area,
each house dressed by
a picket fence guarding
a lush and pretty garden.
I couldn't help thinking about
what Jenni had said about
losing everything, and Mike Bilk
helping them out. This place
was a whole lot of helping out.
I looked over the outside.
The front had bay windows
to the left and right
of the front door.
It looked like a face —
they looked like eyes and the door
looked like a nose, and the porch
like a mouth, a face with no
expression.
I walked slowly up the path
to the door.
Jenni's mum opened the door
to greet me; her face was
red raw and battered by tears.
'Come in, can I get you a drink?
I'm Martha,' she said.
'I know we haven't met before, but

Jenni, she spoke about you, said you were
good friends.'
Martha looked so different
to Jenni, no real resemblance.
Her hair was dark with tight curls, and
you could see the grey was starting to
come through in her roots.
If there was anything to link her
and Jenni it was that they had a similar figure; Martha
looked good for her age.
'How are you holding up?' I said.
'It's been tough,
but we mustn't stop, we can't stop,
not for anything. We must
find her. I know she's not dead.
I must find her.
I've got to make it all right
with her. I've not been there...
for her.'
She went out of the room,
with tears in her eyes.
I looked around the room.
So many pictures,
so many memories,
most covered in a thin layer of dust.
I didn't
know how I felt.
I didn't know what to say.
I called up to say I was leaving, but
I didn't think she heard me.

Then she suddenly appeared
at the top of the stairs with
something in her hand.
The sunlight pierced through
the landing windows,
catching it.
'I wanted to show you this.'
She handed me a photograph
in an ornate frame:
it was her and Jenni
and two guys; one
I assumed was her dad and
the other was Mike Bilk.
He had his hand on Jenni's waist.

HELPING MIKE

'Jenni loved her dad so much,
I think that is why she
is helping Mike.
They were such good friends,
maybe it's like being
with her dad or something.'
I looked closer.
They were standing in front
of a sign – it read:
'Luxury Apartments Coming Soon',
then above it
'Circano'.
I was about to ask her about Stefan, when she
started in:
'And Stefan has been a really good
friend, not a boyfriend.' She was careful
to add this in.
'I think he tries to be all macho, but
really he's been very kind, and I know
he's been helping Jenni with finding
lots of old documents for the campaign.'
This last bit really made my ears prick up.
What documents?

WORK

I start work early, but it's not where
I want to be.
I'm washing dishes, scraping the sinew
of a small carcase smothered
in something that resembles
gravy.
Checking the surfaces are kept clear,
mopping the floors in the kitchen.
This is work; this is how I see it
and how I'd describe it.
From 10 a.m. till 5 p.m.,
checking the surfaces are kept clear,
mopping the floors
and then repeat
and repeat
at this diner,
this little diner
in town.
It's my second year as porter.
The work is mundane
but I like it; mundane is good.
But right now, all I can think about
is Jenni.
I knock off work
and check my phone.
Three missed calls,
all from her,

all from Jenni,
or the person pretending
to be Jenni.
Maybe I should have told them,
Bellucci and Cole. They
could help; they seemed nice.
These phone calls – they must be
someone playing a joke, right?
But I can't tell them. What if she calls again?
It's all I've got left of her.
My only piece of Jenni,
my only link.

PAST AND PRESENT

My head starts spinning again,
like I'm in between here
and then.
The past and present
merging into one.

ON EDGE

I sip some water,
my head hurting again.
I need to know.
I don't think they'll
believe me, I mean,
why should they?
I think they'll think it's me,
it's me that's caused this.
My hands feel clammy
and I'm on edge, but
I know what happened.
I just can't remember.

OBSERVED

I wander back down
the path and away from
the work.
It's getting late, and I want
to get back home.
As I start to trot along the road,
I feel a presence, like I'm
being followed,
watched,
observed.
I look over my shoulder,
and in the distance I
can just make out a figure,
but who could it be?
I wonder if it's Stefan
or the police.
I break into a run, and keep looking over
my shoulder, but the figure appears
the same distance away,
not near enough to make out,
not far enough away to escape.
I can feel my heartbeat
in my neck, pounding
in my neck, my chest,
my temples.
I scramble around the front pocket
of my bag,

trying to put my hands
on my key.
Clasping it tightly,
I aim for the keyhole,
but my hand is trembling
and I keep missing the slot.
I peer down the street
and the figure is still there,
but this time it stands,
like it's waiting.
I turn and try the key again,
but my hands are so sweaty now.
I look again and the figure
has gone,
and at that moment a hand
touches my shoulder.
I turn around and it's Dad
and I take a
deep breath.
'You OK?' he asks.
'Can you hear me?'
And I'm not quite sure.
Dad takes me upstairs;
he can see I'm shaken up.
The house is so cold, I start
to shiver, my hands shaking
a little.
Dad turns the thermostat up on the wall
in the hallway, and the boiler fires up, and
just the thought of the heating

coming on makes me feel warmer.
Dad doesn't say a word;
he just takes my hand and
helps me into bed, shuts
off the light and closes the door.
I listen to him
head down the stairs.

EYES WIDE OPEN

I think of her:
her hair wild and blonde,
her eyes always darting,
alive, frantic and deep blue,
like oceans.
Her body, her legs,
her hands, her breasts.
I would watch her breathe in and out.
It was hypnotic.
I would stare at her ears, which are
almost pixie-like,
their outer part perfectly curved.
It's like I'm dreaming
with my eyes wide open.

VOICES

I wake up to my phone
vibrating and knocking against
the leg of my bed.
I lean down and grab it.
It's Jenni's number; I answer it.
The same deep humming sound
comes out, but the beeping sound
is not as loud as before
and now there is a new sound
and I'm trying to make it out,
but it's distorting; it sounds
like voices; it sounds like lots
of different voices all talking at once
and I can't make out any words.
So I start to shout into the phone,
'Can anyone hear me?
Can anyone hear me?
Who is there?
Who is this?'
Over and over I shout
these things
and then, all of a sudden,
the line goes dead.

GAPS

I start to think again
about Jenni and what happened
that night. I feel helpless,
like I'm not doing enough,
that I'm not finding out enough
information about it all.
I need to do more.
I need to know more.
But how?
My mind just feels so jumbled.
I keep making notes, but there
are so many gaps.

HUMMING

It is 3 a.m.
and my phone begins to ring.
I grab it
and it's her,
it's Jenni.
I fumble trying to answer it.
As I place the phone to my ear,
I can hear a humming,
like a fridge hums
but louder,
the volume turned up.
'Jenni, are you there?' I ask.
Nothing comes back,
just that deep humming,
but the line goes dead.

SLUSH

Rain sheets across
the surface of the street,
washing away any trace
of the snow, the slush,
the dirty slush
staining the street and road.
Cars whistle past and I
feel like I'm floating,
just making my way
along, like I'm not there,
as if I'm watching a movie,
a movie of myself.
I haven't looked at
my phone, not
for a day.
That haunted phone,
haunted by her.
I've got to find it –
find her phone.
Find out what sick fuck
is doing this.
Why would someone do this?
To me, to Jenni.
Wonderful, sweet Jenni,
who never hurt anyone.
But the call, it can't be her,
it can't be Jenni,

not my Jenni.
My Jenni
isn't Jenni any more.
My Jenni, I don't think she's
coming back.

CONNECTED

I decide to
head over to Mike Bilk's building,
to his offices,
his place of work.
I need to get inside and check,
check if he knows anything.
The photo felt like a clue.
Waterside and Jenni's dad.
Were they connected?
Maybe Bilk knows something.

THE TWELFTH FLOOR

The building is a high-rise
and Mike's offices are on the twelfth floor,
according to the list on the doors.
I buzz the reception
and
go up.
Mike's own secretary
greets me at the entrance to
the twelfth floor.
'I told them he's not in today,' she says.
'I've told them three times!
I'm so sorry you had to make your way up here.
He'll be back tomorrow.'
I hang back until she is out of sight,
then slip through the door to the twelfth floor.
Her desk is parallel to a gap in the wall
so I wait, tight against the wall.
I'm sure he is here.

STIFLING

I shuffle with my back
to the wall,
down the corridor.
I hear his secretary, chatting
on the phone.
So I crouch down, and make my way
along, her voice guiding me
under her very nose. I can almost
feel her breath.
The walls are painted off-white
and there are no windows
anywhere; it feels so enclosed and
stifling; so much so, I'm
finding it hard to breathe.
I keep asking myself, What am I doing?
This isn't me, I'm not this person.
Not the hero. I am a nobody;
I'm not the one to do anything
about anything.
And why for her?
What was it about her?
Why did she beguile me?
I can only think it is because no girl
had ever shown me attention before, not really.
I love her
more than anything.
And that is why,
why I have to find out.

DEEP BREATH

Once I'm past her, I get back
on my feet and walk,
back against the wall, until
I reach his office door,
his name emblazoned on it.
I hear a voice…
It's very low, hard to define.
'Just put this thing to bed, would you?
Someone brings it up everywhere
I go.'
I turn the handle and step inside.
Mike Bilk
sits behind his desk and takes
the receiver away from his ear.
'How did you get in here?' he asks.
'Who are you? What do you want?'
I take a deep breath.
'I'm Hobart, Hobs. I'm a friend of
Jenni Beaumont.'
'Jenni Beaumont? Oh, I'm sorry, I…' He pauses.
He places the receiver back to his ear.
'Look, I'll call you back. Something
has come up.'
I look round the office: books
and files are wall to wall
and big old oil paintings.
'I was sorry to hear about her going missing – nice

girl, good kid,' he says.
'But what can I do for you?'
'I just wanted to know...
did Jenni do some work for you?'
'Er... she delivered a few leaflets
for our campaign, but that's all.
Why?' he asks.
'Just curious.
I'm just trying to put a few
things together.'
'Well, I think you should probably leave
that type of thing to the police. Now,
if you'll excuse me, I have a lot of
work to do and you need to get back.'
He is just like he is on TV,
smug and patronising.
'I need to find her.
I think you might know
where she is.' My voice has begun to rise.
'Look, I don't know why you think I—'
I cut him off.
'Circano!' I shout.
Mike Bilk clears his throat, this time talking
much more slowly, with a resurgent
authority.
'Look, kid' –
the word 'kid', trying to make me feel small
and insignificant –
'let me try and explain
something to you.

In medieval times,
the kings of Europe didn't
answer to their people, they
only answered to God. Do you
know what this meant?'
I just shrug my shoulders, his
eyes fixed on mine.
'It meant total obedience.
Those kings were God's
representatives, his vessels –
do you understand
what I'm saying, Hobs?'
I nod nervously, his eyes
bearing down on me, the words
ringing in my ears.
'I'm sure Jenni is fine; probably
just skipped town for a few days
to stay with friends.
Now, if there is nothing else
I can help you with, I think
it would be best if you left now.'
And that's exactly what I do.

THE LAST TIME

I think of the last time
I saw her,
when she said,
'I've got so much else going on right now.'

MISSED CALLS

I'm sitting on my bed
and I look at my phone,
when I see the missed
calls from Jenni's phone.
So many missed calls, all
the time I was in that office.
Like warning signals. Why didn't I push
him more?
Then it buzzes again in my hand,
before I can even get it up to my ear;
the beeping sound is so loud
I feel like my ear will burst.
It goes right through me.
It's at that moment that I feel
a pain in my head.
I keep thinking I should
go to the police,
but Mike's words
sting my thoughts.

COMING OUT TO PLAY

The pain
gets more and more intense.
My eyes sting.
I feel like I'm stumbling around,
blind drunk.
I look at my watch: time is
getting on. I look out of my window.
I look up to the end of the road –
it seems a mile away – and there
is something else up there,
something standing in my way,
motionless,
in darkness,
a figure,
that same figure
from before. I think about
calling out,
shouting at it, but what if it's
the police? I'm sure
they think I'm involved somehow
in why Jenni went missing.
Whoever it is is giving
me the creeps.

THE OTHER SIDE

I look across to the other side
of the street, watching the figure
as it goes; it seems to grow
as I move.
The whirring of vehicles.
My heart is thumping so hard, I
think it might burst straight
out of my chest.
I see the figure drift across
to the same side of the street.
Above my eye the pain
is searing so much, I shut
my eyes.
I prise them open
and the figure is gone.
I start to walk tentatively across the landing.
The light outside is fading,
fading fast.
I peer through the window at the far end,
following my ears,
following the sound
of the vehicles,
of the trucks...
... vans,
combing the streets.
Through the window I see
the street light up

with flashes in the distance
and the sound of sirens
increasing like turning
a volume dial,
and the panic increases, my head
throbbing more than before.
More than I've ever known.
I can hardly breathe, hardly
stand up.
I stumble downstairs and
look through the glass pane on the door, and
there
is the figure,
and it's getting closer.

REVERBERATE

I'm running back through the house,
through the back gate,
down the road,
not looking back.
I'm running like I'm
never going to stop.
Forward...
that's all I can think about.
The sound of hissing
tyres reverberate around
me as cars race along
the road in front of me.
I reach the crossing
and I rapidly tap on the button
to change the lights – so many
cars.
And it's still there, getting closer
and closer, the figure growing
ever bigger...
... nearer.
The light goes from green
to amber
to red; cars shudder to a stop
as I bolt across the road, not looking
back again, just focusing
on moving forward.
Rain begins to splatter on the ground,

getting heavier with
each stride; drips flow
down my face, into my eyes
and I can barely see.
I'm running blindly
to get back home.
I see lights
like spots in front of me,
to the side
and above, spotlights
flickering
on
and off.
On and off.
My eyes sting
with each
flicker, the pain
inching its way
to the back of my head
and back again.

HAZY

The next week felt hazy.
I think we
all knocked on doors.
Putting up posters.
Doing press interviews.
Jonas.
Tam.
Mia.
Teachers.
Neighbours.
Locals.
Even Stefan Bilk
and Mike Bilk
were all over the news,
Mike using it as a platform,
as another one of his moments.
I wished I could just stop all this.
Find her.
Bring her back.
We made lists of places
where she might go, where
she might have chosen to go.
But we could only find blanks…
… dead ends.
We scanned crowds,
we knocked on more doors.
We tried to read blank faces, but

nothing.
So many people go missing, lost.
Far away or under your nose.
Running from something.
Leaving something behind, leaving
people behind...
troubles... feelings...
guilt... fears...
a situation, a time...
a place.

ONE BY ONE

First Rita,
then Mia,
then Tam,
then Stefan Bilk.
I passed by them one by one
throughout the day.
I passed Raoul,
I passed Jonas,
then Mia,
then Tam,
then Rita,
then Raoul,
then Stefan Bilk.
Throughout the day
I saw faces.
I passed them by;
they passed by me.
Faster
and faster
... and faster,
again
and again.

BUCKLING

I feel like throwing up,
trying to make progress
up this street, trying to get away.
Adrenaline pumping through me,
fuelling me.
And I'm back on my street,
looking straight at
my front door.
It's so close.
So near. But I don't want it to be.
But I'm broken.
Buckling in this moment.
Then I'm through the door,
slamming it shut behind me.
My heavy breathing begins
to recede, to fade.
The house is dark now,
reflecting the outside.
I head to the kitchen,
still catching my breath,
and winning.
Opening the fridge door.
My face embraces the coolness
from within and as my eyes adjust
to the light inside, I grab
some juice
and glug the entire carton.

The sound of humming from
the fridge begins
to fade as I close the door.

EVERY BIT

Feelings were raw,
for everyone, but for me
they were abrasions, shredding
every piece...
every bit...
every thought.
And fear...
I had so much fear...
fear that I might never see
her again.
When Mum left, the pain was
so intense, so hard to deal with.
I couldn't lose love again, not
like that.
I was fourteen the day Mum left.
I got back from school,
and I knew as soon as I
walked through the door she'd gone.
Things were missing in the house,
just little things, little ornaments from the
sideboards, nothing valuable,
just stuff that was hers, really hers.
Dad was sitting in their
bedroom looking lost, behind him
all the drawers of the dresser
left hanging open, each one empty.
These are the only details.

He sat holding his guitar,
trying to strum out a tune.
It sounded discordant,
unpleasant to the ears. I couldn't
figure it out at the time,
but I guess he was trying
to create something in that moment,
a piece of music to exorcise
the pain.
We never spoke about
that day and
that's all I really remember
from the day she left, but
I wish we could talk.
It might help
us both.

GET SOME SLEEP

I wake up lying on the floor of the kitchen.
The front door opens
and it's Dad coming back from work.
He helps me to my feet.
'Breakfast?' he asks.
I shake my head.
'Get some sleep,' he goes.
I head to the stairs...
... to my bedroom.
I look at Dad.
He says,
'Get some sleep.'

LIGHTS, CAMERA, ACTION

Lights... camera... action
on repeat,
day after day, and
there was nothing.
No sign.
No clues.
Only darkness in a world
with very little light.
We headed to school;
we resumed our 'normal' lives.
English lessons with an empty seat.
Lunchtime with no one to
share it with.
The others just carried on,
same old cliques doing the same old things,
day in...
... day out.
Like they'd already forgotten her.
When somebody goes missing, the first
forty-eight hours are key.
Establishing the levels of risk; I
read all about it.
The police identify hazards,
what ifs, what buts.
Speed and scale of search are advised
by level of hazards, vulnerability.
I read about it.

Jenni was considered low to medium,
not high.
Her age,
her circumstances.
All low to medium.
I read all about it.
It had been two weeks now,
nearly three.

CONFIDE

I was in the principal's office.
She'd called me in for a 'chat'.
'How are you holding up?'
I looked up at the ceiling.
The fan above me was still and dusty.
'I know you are very fond of Jenni.'
I acknowledged her with a smile.
'We can help you if you want to talk
about it, confide in someone. We can help
with that… we want to help with that.'
I looked back up at the fan; I wondered
when they last turned it on.
'Just so you know,
we are all here for you,
all the staff, everyone,
we are all here for you.'
I liked the words, but somehow
they didn't seem sincere.
Heading down the corridor, I passed
the lockers…
mine…
Jenni's.
I headed into the toilets,
then the cubicle.

I sat down,
looking at the door.

THE CUBICLE

I was remembering that place.
We'd been there before, Jenni
and I.
We'd snuck out of class
just to get some privacy.
We didn't really talk,
just held each other and
kissed.
I remember looking
in her eyes
and she moved
her head towards
my ear
and breathed out the words,
and my back tingled
and my groin ached.
'I'm here.'

I'M HERE

I'd studied the various
messages, pictures of dicks,
random names, numbers, graffiti
at its best.
But in amongst those totems of youth
it had caught my eye:
two simple words,
together
in a line.
'I'm here.'
And it was in Jenni's writing.

ZAP

The doorbell rings,
breaking the memories,
and I glimpse through the
closed curtains to the street below.
It's Tam.
She looks upset.
I shout down, but
she doesn't seem to hear me.
I place the phone on my bed
and go to the door.
She comes straight in,
brushing past me
without saying a word,
her eyes blood-red from tears.
I go to sit next to her
but I feel a zap in my head
like an electric current passing
through it.
Then I'm back in my room, looking at
the phone again, not knowing
what is going on.
Then the doorbell rings
and I look again through the gap
in the curtains
and there is no one there.
And I'm back with my memories again.

RECOUNTING THE WORDS

I combed the cubicle.
Where was she?
Recounting the words:
'I'm...
... here.'
Here? Those simple words
that meant so much
when she uttered them to me.
I kept hearing them,
like they were coming from right beside me.
Was there something in the place
of her?
I started reaching round the bowl
that was wet with stale piss,
stale piss
and crap and crusted bits
of toilet paper.
Then I felt it.
I felt something...
taped to the back of the pipe.
I ripped it off.
In my hand was a phone.
I immediately switched it on.
Would this help me find her?
So many questions...
so many thoughts.
The screen was black

and as I swiped to open it
to the home screen,
no apps, just a background picture.
It was a painting…
of a king.
And a folder
called
'Circano Files'.

DIZZY

I'm feeling dizzy now,
so I sit back down on the bed.
I reach down to look at the phone,
Jenni's phone,
but it's powered down, so
I reconnect it to the charger,
and as I do, my own phone
starts to ring.
It's Jenni's phone.

DÉJÀ VU

The doorbell rings again.
It is Tam.
This moment on repeat.
I place the phone back on my bed
and go to the door.
She comes straight in;
she doesn't say a word,
her eyes blood-red from tears,
her face inches from mine.
Another zap in my head.
Back in my room again, looking at
the phone, not knowing
what is going on.
I can hear a sound coming from the phone,
so I put it
to my ear. The pain in my head
comes back and the beeping sound
is louder than ever, pulsing through me.
I try to pull it away, but like a magnet
it keeps pulling back.
Muffled sounds start to drown
out the beeping, and an array of
different voices. I can't make out
what they are saying,
what they are shouting, what
sounds like a commotion.
Suddenly the phone goes dead

and I'm back by the curtains
looking out
at nothing.

PLANS

She must have planned this...
and if she'd planned this,
she must have planned it
before.
She took the time to come here; she
took the time to wipe her phone
and set it up so I had a clue,
just one. Some files, documents
I'd never seen before.
Why couldn't she have just left a note?
Or emailed it to me?
Not this espionage shit!
I didn't know what do to with this.
I felt so angry right then.
Was this some sort game?
If it was, I didn't want to play
any more.
I stormed out of the cubicle,
out of the toilets,
down the hall, and
out through the entrance.
I pushed past Jonas, who was
hanging around outside.
'What's the deal, bro?' he said.
'Not now.'
And I was then running...
... sprinting, but I didn't know
where to.

TEAR ON A TEAR

A tear on a tear
on a tear...
The whole situation becoming
alive in my head: not that
it wasn't before, but now
I was fully aware of what
was going on, that Jenni
may never come back.
That Jenni might be...
... dead.
Walking past some shops,
I saw Mike Bilk on a bunch of TV
screens being interviewed.
Each screen bigger than the next.
Twenty-one inches,
Mike Bilk's face.
Thirty-two inches,
Mike Bilk's eyes.
Thirty-seven inches,
the interviewer's right ear.
Forty inches,
Mike Bilk's office.
Forty-three inches,
Mike's Bilk's office wall.
Forty-nine inches.

HEAVY AND PAINFUL

My head is so heavy and painful,
my heart raging in my chest, bursting
to get out.
Each new memory that comes brings
more pain, more discomfort.
It feels unbearable now, but I can't stop: I have
to keep going, probing my mind
for what comes next.

STRUCK ME

What does Mike Bilk know?
What has Mike Bilk done?
This must be something to do
with him, the picture on the phone.
It was bothering me. I felt like I'd seen
it before, or something like it.
Then it struck me.
Mike Bilk's office.

UNCOMFORTABLE

I ran through the reception,
pushing past anyone in my way.
'Where is he?' I said.
His secretary leaned back,
looking uncomfortable.
'He's not here right now.'
'Where is he?'
This time with my hands face down
on her desk, my palms pushed into
the oak veneer and my eyes
locked on to hers.
'He really isn't here, not this time.'
That was when I burst into his office
and it was empty,
but there
was the wall behind his desk with a painting on it,
a painting just beyond his empty chair.
A painting
of a king,
the same as the one
on Jenni's phone.
I opened the phone again
and clicked on the photo.
Nothing happened.
I opened the files folder,
then clicked on the images tab.
A whole bunch of thumbnail images

scattered across the screen.
They looked like documents,
so I clicked the top-left-
hand-corner one, which opened
instantly.
It was an invoice
and at the top it said:
'Waterside'.
And at the bottom was
a signature.
I could just about make out the name
… Mike Bilk.

INFORMATION

Was this what Jenni
was talking about?
The information she was looking for?
My head was spinning;
I needed to get my
head straight.

LEAVING

I left, knocking over a plant pot
that shattered all over the floor,
with bits of soil splattered across
the cream carpet, which
I accidentally trod
in as I went.
Back on the street
rain had started sleeting
across the path.
Traffic slowed and started
to build. I stood by the lights
waiting to cross.
The lights blinked
from green
to amber
to red.
I walked head down.
Emotions started to rise in me,
anger turning to sadness.
Tears streamed down my face;
people walked past, looking at me,
but nobody stopped,
nobody asked.
Nobody at all.
What had he done with
Jenni?
I needed more answers

and I needed them
right then.

GULPING

I'm back downstairs.
I stop, standing bent double,
trying to catch my breath,
gulping for air, grabbing only
a little each time.
It feels like the closer
I get to remembering what happened,
the worse I feel.
I hope Dad comes home soon.
I think I need to go to
the doctor's.

PRODUCTION-LINE HOUSE

I stood in front of the Bilks' house,
the grand house that Mike built.
It sat in a quiet suburb, away
from real life, away from real people.
The house was a new house,
a production-line house, the
same as all the others
in the road.
Each as grand as the next.
The windows at the front
were huge and from the
bottom of the drive you
could just make out
the opulent interior
of the living room, large
plasma TV, leather corner sofa,
white walls.
Everything was white, made
to look slick
and clean
and pure.
This place looked like something
out of a magazine.
But like the fancy
cars that sat on the drive,
it had no soul, it
had no character; it perfectly

represented its owners.
I took a couple of deep breaths
and started up the drive.

FROM AFAR

I banged my fist on the door.
I heard Andrea Bilk slurring and mumbling
as she unbolted it.
I'd only seen her from afar
or on TV, but she was more attractive
in the flesh; she was well dressed
and it was clear
she still took pride in her
appearance, trying to distract people from
looking below the surface.
'Where is he?'
'Where's who?' she asked.
'Mike.'
'He's not here… He's never here!' she said.
She stumbled back, allowing me in.
'Who are you?'
'I'm Hobs, I'm Jenni Beaumont's boyfriend.'
She started to laugh.
'Jenni Beaumont? Ha, boyfriend?
That little bitch.
Which one are you?' she said.

COMFORTABLE

It's several hours
until I wake up. Dad
must have been and gone.
He's put a blanket over me,
almost covering my head, and
a cool flannel on my brow.
It feels good: comfortable, cosy, warm.
I see the two phones on the coffee table
beside the sofa, side by side.
Jenni's and mine,
side by side.
And they both start to ring
at the same time.

DUMB KID

Andrea Bilk grabbed a bottle
from the kitchen
and ushered me in with it.
'You poor kid, you poor dumb kid.
You really didn't know?'
She poured from the bottle into
a glass tumbler, almost filling it, then
she necked the whole lot. Her eyes
seemed to spin as she did.
'Know what?' I shouted. 'Tell me.'
'She and Mike, you know... are very good friends,' she said.
'And more than!'
I shook my head, the information not really
penetrating.
'And now the silly girl, well, she's gone.'
'Where is she?' I said. 'You know, don't you?'
I grabbed hold of Andrea Bilk; I started to shake her
over and over, louder and louder:
'Where is she?'

TWO PHONES

I don't want to answer either
of them, but the ringing becomes
incessant, and I feel that pain again
in my head. Just need to close my eyes,
ease the pain,
but each pocket is empty.
I look around the room, and the walls
are now spinning, and the light
on the ceiling is flickering
and pulsing, growing brighter.
The pain in my head is coming
in waves, in time with the ringing.
I grab both phones,
mine
and Jenni's,
and start to smash them on the floor.
Bits of phone flying across the room, but
the ringing doesn't stop
and the light in the room is getting so bright
I can't keep my eyes open.
Suddenly the entire room goes dark.

POWER AND INFLUENCE

Shrugging me aside, Andrea
refilled her glass and necked another.
'I haven't done anything to her.
I might have had a quiet word with her…
tell her who she's dealing with.'
'Who she's dealing with?
You're just a drunk,
with a shitty husband.'
'My husband is everything – he's everything
to this town, this place, this city. My husband
is a gift to this place; my husband is a
king in this place,' she yelled.
'Is that what you tell yourself?'
'That's the truth,
and nothing, not even that little whore
is going to stop him, not now, not ever. I
won't allow it, so we had a little talk, her
and me…'
I wondered how much of this
vitriol was about the stuff Jenni knew,
or was something else going on?
How far had Jenni gone
to get this information?
She poured another drink, then another,
offered me the bottle, then started up again.
'Power doesn't come from people.' Her
voice was slurring more with each drink.

'It doesn't come from words or deeds; it comes
from loyalty, greed;
it comes from higher places than us,
and he's the most powerful
man in town.'
Her words were mirroring his.
'But you'll never understand that.
You'll never have what he has –
you want to know why?
Why she sees what she sees,
what we all see in him.'
And I looked at her quizzically.
'She's not the first; she won't be the last –
it's what he does.
I've found my way to deal with it.' And she clinked
her glass against a bottle.
'What about Waterside?' my voice raised
more than I thought.
'What about Waterside? Her daddy signed
those papers; her darling daddy was at
fault there.' She smirked.
'And after everything we did for that family.'
'The papers Jenni's dad signed?' I asked.
'Oh, you poor boy, didn't you know?
There's nothing on Mike: his name wasn't
on those papers. You'll learn very quickly
in life about power and influence:
these are what we all cling to,
people like me, like her, like the others.
We crave it, and he delivers.

Wake up, kid.'
I felt worn out,
hoping the lesson was nearly over.
I couldn't trust Andrea with
the things I'd discovered.
'Nothing has happened to that little tramp.
She'll be back, and it won't destroy us.
Nobody will ever destroy
this family – not her, not you, not
anybody!
Now get the hell out of my house.'
A shiver ran down my spine.
I felt like such a fool,
the last to know.

PUSHING

I pushed past her and headed
to the front door. Next to the
door at eye level was a key rack.
There were two sets of car keys. I grabbed both
and headed back through the house,
pushing past Andrea again.
'Hey, where are you going?'
I went out the back of the house
and into the garage through
the side door.
Inside was the car, blue and sporty,
the one I'd seen before.
The car I was now going to use
to find Mike Bilk.
I pressed the key fob
and the lock on the door
pinged up.
I pulled open the door
and I was in.

CALLING HER NAME

There's a low buzzing sound
on the other end
and a voice
and it sounds like it's saying,
'Clear…
Clear…
Clear…'
Over and over.
And I'm shouting
now, calling her name:
'Jenni?
Jenni?
Are you there? Jenni, are you there?
Jenni, are you hurt?
Jenni, please, are you hurt, Jenni?
Jenni, are you OK?
Jenni can you hear me?
Jenni, answer me, please.
Jenni!'

PULL AWAY

The car was low on petrol
but I thought it would be enough.
I really revved the engine, so
the neighbours heard as I pulled
away from the drive,
heading to the pool rooms.
I wanted to see Stefan Bilk.

MOMENT

[ˈməʊm(ə)nt]

Noun

A very brief period of time:
a point in time.

An occasion.
This occasion.
Our moment.

FOCUS

'Clear...'
The sound echoes around my ear,
around the room.
The darkness in the room
seems to lift, and as my eyes
adjust, I start to see figures
appear around me, dark figures,
like the figure I've seen before,
the figure that's been following me,
haunting me,
slowly coming into focus, and I hear
more voices now, so many more.
It all goes dark;
it all goes to nothing.
I'm aware of myself, but I can't
hear or feel...
... or see.
And I feel cold.
I can see so many
moments right now, so
vivid, like I'm reaching
the end.

DOWNLOAD

I pulled into the car park,
and jumped right out. Jonas
was by the entrance, as ever.
'Nice wheels, dude,' he said.
'Not now, J. Is Stefan in there?'
'Yeah, man, by the back tables.'
I handed Jonas the phone.
'Download the image files, J. Put
them on every news site, Twitter, Facebook,
Instagram, everywhere you can,' I commanded.
'What is it, dude? Better not be dick pics!'
'Just do it, J, please.' I was pleading this time.
'Sure, man.'
I headed inside and straight to the back.
I grabbed a cue on the way
and smashed it in half across
the table. Stefan jumped back.
He shoved me hard and I clattered
to the floor, while he tried to head
towards the entrance. I stuck out an arm,
catching his left leg on the calf,
sending him sprawling.
Now standing over him, I wrestled
him to his feet.
'Where is he?' I shouted, holding
the broken end of the cue
up to his face; the end was splintered

and sharp.
I could see he was struggling to speak,
his usual confidence ebbing away.
I shuffled back a little
and he swallowed hard
before finding his voice again.
'He knows where she is.
He's going to give her some money to
stop her talking, sort the problem.
He's meeting her in town,
at the coffee house.'
The same place we usually met –
how ironic…
'How long have you known?' I said.
'I didn't know, not before.
I knew Dad was up to something, but I didn't know
it was to do with Jenni, I swear.
Look, I've told the police everything.
They came to see me just a few hours ago.
Everyone knows she's safe.
We just wanted to expose Dad.
What he did, it was wrong. My mum –
she deserves better.'
Everyone knew
except me!
I threw down the cue
and I was gone.

SLOW MOTION

I'm in slow motion:
movement that is slower.
Movement that is slower than normal.

LOVES ME

It was starting to get darker,
driving down the road.
Not knowing what I'd say to him,
to her...
... to Jenni.
My Jenni, not his.
She loved me, not him.
I knew she did.
She said she did
and I believed her, and I knew
we could sort this out,
make things right again.
For her,
for me,
for us.

HEAVY EYES

My eyes, still adjusting,
feel heavy,
but the figures are closing in
around me
and I'm scrambling on the floor
trying to get away, but I can't get up.
And suddenly, before me, I can
see a road. I'm heading down it
so fast, my eyes can't keep up,
my heavy eyes.

DECIPHER

I spotted them almost immediately,
right where Stefan said they'd be,
over by the café, talking.
I slowed down and turned into a vacant space,
a way back from them.
I sat trying to read their lips,
decipher,
watching her body language,
watching his.
She looked upset; he looked angry.
They began to move away
from the café, trying to look
inconspicuous, not there.
But they were there. I'd seen them
and I decided it was time.

CLEAR...

The road goes on and on.
The figures around me
are closing in,
edging towards me.
I writhe around the floor,
my mind going berserk.
I start to see bright light, like
a spot in the distance, gradually getting bigger
and bigger, till it's all I can see before me.
All I can hear is someone saying,
'Clear...'

ACCELERATOR

My eyes followed as they walked along the street,
heading towards traffic lights near
the railway crossing.
I pulled out into the road and pushed hard
onto the accelerator,
hoping to catch sight of them as they crossed,
hoping they would catch sight of me.
The car picked up pace so quickly; it was
power flowing through me.
Then, from nowhere, a small child
ran from her mother,
tripped into the road,
and I swerved, just missing her.
Then, trying to slam my foot hard onto the brakes,
the car turning and lifting up on one side,
I'd lost control, complete control, all
I could see in front of me was the faces
of Jenni and Mike Bilk, halfway over the crossing.
I was helpless, time standing still
as the car careered straight past them,
over the bridge.

BACK AND FORTH

The light begins to fade.
I'm in a hospital ward. There
are empty beds to the left
and empty beds to the right.
Over the other side of the room
is a group of nurses rushing around,
and a man and a woman, who I assume are doctors,
are barking instructions.
They both look familiar to me, like I've
seen them before.
My mind goes back and forth
from what's real
to what isn't real.
There is a clock above the bed
they are working around.
It reads 20:47.
I decide to walk over, see what's going on.
One of the nurses brushes past me, almost
through me, her hands covered in blood.
I follow her as she walks from the room
and I notice the room is windowed
and there are some people
standing looking in.
I recognise them: each one is someone I know.
Jonas, Tam,
and next to them is Jenni,
tears streaming down her face.

I rush over, pushing my face against
the window.
'Jenni, it's me. I'm here, I'm here,' I go,
frantically banging on the glass between us,
but she doesn't hear me,
and she doesn't see me.
I see two more nurses rush in
with a trolley; it has some kind of machine on it.
I follow them back to the bed
where the female doctor is giving the person
a heart massage, her arms thrusting
up and down, counting to fifteen,
up and down.
I move in closer to see who is on the bed.
The whir of ambulances, police cars, fire engines
can be heard all around the town.
The car is on its roof, flipped over.
Mike Bilk is sitting several metres away,
breathing heavily, shaken
but alive.
Unhurt.
I'm no longer in the car.
The broken, crumpled car.
All I can see is smoke
and debris,
scattered around like confetti.
The sound has been put on mute.
I see
but I don't hear.
I think

but I don't feel.
Fumes spew from the back
and front of the car;
glass lies all around
the floor in front of me,
little pieces glistening in
light like diamonds.
I see pairs of feet darting
about, and different faces
looking into my eyes.
I see their mouths
moving
but I hear nothing.
Everything in slow motion;
everything feels unreal...
... a dream.
Shards of twisted metal
lie a few feet away.
I'm lying here watching,
but I feel nothing
and I can't move
or speak.

JOLT

The male doctor readies
the machine that beeps
and then he places two pads
on the chest of the person. There's a sudden jolt
and I'm back in my house,
feeling like my mind is
clear and engaged.
Then another jolt.
I'm back on the ward.
Jolt.
I'm in college. Jolt.
Back in the ward.
I'm shaking my head, twitching,
not knowing what's going on.
Back in the ward, I'm scrambling to get
to the bed, trying to get someone's
attention, get someone's help.
Charge, BEEPppp.
Jolt.
With Jenni, in the cubicle, memories
coming and going.
Charge, BEEPppp, jolt.
The ward again, now fighting my way
to the bed, to see who is there, to see what is happening.
And then they part
like I'm Moses parting the Red Sea.
I hear the male doctor go,

'I'm gonna call it at nine p.m. exactly –
everyone OK with that?'
They all nod, some more reluctantly than others.
The female doctor looks over.
'I really thought he'd make it... he was looking
good there for a while,' she says.

THE WHIRRING

The whirring from the machine as it de-charges
sounds like the hum of the security
vehicles outside. Was any of that real?
I'm starting to freak out, feel really scared.
Jenni, she's alive, but I held her in my arms
by the side of the road.
I held her; she lay by my feet.
But she's screaming through the glass over where I'm
standing.
I look back over at the bed, now no one is around it.
I can see…
I can see clearly.
I can see the person on the bed
and it's me.
It's me on the bed, me
lying there, with not much air
left in my lungs, no blood
pumping through my veins.
Just a body, or a corpse, with
a soul, a voyeur
of the whole thing.
This nurse comes over,
a male nurse, older than the others.
He's got a dish with water in
and begins to wash away the blood
from my head,
my body's head.

I can see tears roll down his
cheeks. It's my dad.
My dad, and he's been here all along.
The first thing that
is real that I've seen all night.
He is working tonight.
He always works nights.
And he's doing his job.

SORRY

The circus has died down
and only Jenni remains.
She sits by my side now
and I feel a vibration
in my hand. Looking down,
I see a phone, Jenni's phone.
I press the answer button
and hear an automated message.
'You have one new message,
message from—' and I hear her voice,
'Jenni.'
And look over at her.
She's leaning in
and as she starts to
whisper in my ear,
I hear her.
I hear her voice
coming from the phone.
'I'm sorry,' is the first thing she says.
Over and over.
'I'm sorry, I'm sorry.
What were you doing?
What were you thinking?' she goes.
I try to respond, but nothing comes out.
I'm mute, silent, but I can still feel
my stomach twisting…
turning.

TRUTH

She tells me everything.
She tells me about getting close to Mike.
'He was charming. He made me
feel useful, needed. He seemed to
know how I wanted to feel
and made it all happen. I
was a fool – stupid, giddy
teenager. He worked me,
like he works everybody.
I don't think I was the only one,
looking at the way he looked
and acted around the interns.
Then I was staying behind,
sorting out the post,
and this unmarked package came
for him, so I opened it,
as I do all the post when
I'm in the office.
It had all these documents
about Circano, mainly invoices
and planning papers. They all
had sign-offs from Mike Bilk,
but the authorities
had always said it was my dad,
that Mike Bilk was just a small
shareholder.' She starts crying.
'He'd forged the papers,

I don't know how.'
But he'd set up her dad
on the Circano deal.
'I never slept with him,
but the pressure was there and
he said he'd make it difficult for me
and my mum, how he'd got us
a home and could so easily take it away again.
He thought we needed him and that empowered him.
I just started distancing myself
after that; eventually I just had to get away.
I am sorry to put you through that.
I thought I'd just sort my shit out
then confront him. I
never wanted to involve you.
There were too many of them
involved already.
I was just so scared, desperate.'
She tells me it was Stefan
who sent the package,
Stefan who sent
the documents,
Stefan who was so sick
of what his father had done,
sick of the way his dad
treated his mum.
It was Stefan who
found the papers
before Mike could destroy
them; he knew he had to

bide his time with them,
wait for the opportune
moment. Jenni was it.
'And the phone, that was a back-up,
plan B, a substitute if we went into extra time,
insurance. I don't think I ever
truly wanted you to find it.'
What is real and what isn't
don't seem to matter.
What is now is all
I want.
And maybe one day a baby...
the baby growing inside her
that's ours, a family
of us.
She tells me the truth.
She was there in the coffee shop
to tell Mike
all she knew.
How it was him that had
driven her dad to take his life.
And she's sorry,
so sorry, so, so sorry, for
not telling me and for going away,
for hiding, for not talking to me.
'His actions left us with nothing:
penniless, without a husband, without a father.
He took that from us.' So
she headed up east. She stayed with an old friend
just to get away, to figure it out,

but she didn't tell a soul, not me,
not her mum,
and she didn't meant to cause so
much trouble, with police being involved
and people searching. It was never meant
to be this way,
any of it. She just wanted to expose him
for what he is.
And I can feel tears, even though
there are none on my face,
but I can see hers.
She leans in.
'You asked me a while ago
about the story I made up
about you when I
saw you, my people-watching story of you.
Well.' She pauses
and takes a deep breath.
'You were so much better than the story.'

THE KING IS DEAD

Mike Bilk's daily ritual is being
surrounded by flashing lights
and police and security,
his face scratched
and flushed. This is the end.
The end of this part of his story.
It's the end of the story for all
of us. The story of us
is over.
His power gone,
his influence gone, he's this week's
scandal, the media's new whipping boy.
Through these eyes I see it all.
Through these eyes I feel some sense
of triumph, even though my
achievement now feels like
I've stepped onto foreign land.
The king is dead, along with
his divine right to rule.

BEFORE

Lying on the ground, my head
resting on her lap.
My eyes so heavy, they close…
    I try to prise them open.
They'll be here soon
   and they will ask questions,
lots of questions.
Lying on the ground
with the body of the boy she knew…

HEAD IS IN HIS HANDS

I can see Dad,
just about make him out.
He's sitting on the edge
of the bed.
His head is in his hands.
I think he is crying.
Is this the ending?
Just behind him
is someone else,
someone I haven't seen
in a long time.
He gets up again and wipes
my brow and I'm back in my bath.
I'm three years old. I'm playing
with some crappy plastic toys…
then I'm six and Dad is cutting my hair,
the flecks of hair falling into the water.
Then I'm me a week ago.
I'm on my own,
all alone,
and the tap drips slowly,
slowly… slowly.

AND WE'RE DANCING

Then I'm with Dad and Mum,
and Dad is playing his guitar
and we're dancing
around the living room
of our old house.
And then I'm back here,
looking at all this.
Now I'm in my room,
Dad sitting at the end
of my bed,
looking at me.
And then I'm back here
again, and he's doing the same.
I'm here, in this place,
neither alive
nor dead.
I see things,
hear things,
but that is all.
One day I hope it will come
so I don't have to see
these things or live these things again,
this limbo, this ambiguity.
I hope one day I might see my child,
our child.
The child that we could've had.

NO FAIRY TALE

This is no fairy tale.
It's pain,
it's confusion.
But I will take it all
for these few moments
if that is what this is, as the final
gusts of air start to escape my lungs,
to see her face,
the face of the girl I love,
the girl who loves me.
My girl.
Jenni.
That's when the bleeping starts,
the monitor with its leads
attached to my chest, kicking into life.
People in the room start
scurrying around;
light flashes in my eyes
as one of them lifts the lid of
each eye, flashing a torch in them.
I keep switching back and forth
from being on the bed
to seeing myself.
That's when I inhale a deep breath
of air.
That's when I open my eyes.
And I don't know where I am.

ACKNOWLEDGEMENTS

This book wouldn't have been published without the support and encouragement of my wonderful agent Becky Bagnell, the team at Unbound, Katy Guest, DeAndra Lupu. Thank you for the wonderful, insightful editing by Roisin Heycock, you always make my writing so much better; to Kate Quarry for the copy editing; and to Hayley Shepherd for the proofreading.

Huge thanks to my family and friends who have always given me the support, love and encouragement when I need it the most. To my amazing, generous Twitter family, I'm so grateful to be connected to so many incredible people. To the Bacas crew for a comforting place for me to do re-writes.

Grateful to David Lynch and Raymond Chandler for creating amazing work.

All my love to Michelle, Eli and Sonny – you truly are the best.

A NOTE ON THE AUTHOR

GILES PALEY-PHILLIPS is the author of nine children's books, including *The Fearsome Beastie* (Maverick Arts Publishing), which won the People's Book Prize 2012 and the Heart of Hawick Children's Book Award 2013. His book *Little Bell and the Moon* (Fat Fox) was shortlisted for the People's Book Prize 2016 and longlisted for the North Somerset Teachers' Book Award 2015. His semi-autobiographical novel *One Hundred and Fifty-Two Days*, published in 2020, was his first book for adults.

Giles has appeared on *Good Morning Britain* and an author special of BBC2's *Eggheads*, and was a judge on ITV's *Share a Story*. He also writes regular book columns for *Title* and *Aquila* magazines, and is the producer and co-host of the British Podcast Awards-nominated iTunes Top 10 podcast *BLANK*.

Giles lives in Seaford, East Sussex, with his wife, Michelle, and their two sons, Elijah and Sonny. He is a patron for Action Aid UK.

@ELIISTENDER10

Unbound is the world's first crowdfunding publisher, established in 2011.

We believe that wonderful things can happen when you clear a path for people who share a passion. That's why we've built a platform that brings together readers and authors to crowdfund books they believe in – and give fresh ideas that don't fit the traditional mould the chance they deserve.

This book is in your hands because readers made it possible. Everyone who pledged their support is listed below. Join them by visiting unbound.com and supporting a book today.

Nathalie Adam
Julia Alexander
Eluned Allen
Jill Allen
Kendra Alvey
Debbie Androlia
Gordon Archbold
Richard Astill
Paul Attwell
Taj Atwal
Hellen Bach
Anki Backman
Becky Bagnell
Sarah Bailey
Rachel Bailey-Hogg
Tony Baines
Joan Ballantyne
Alison Barber
Marie Barker
Andrea Barlien
Becky Barnes
Athena Barrett
Mo Bateman

Gail Beach
Samantha Beaton
Dina Bedwell
Georgina Belcher
Jo Bell
Joanna Bell
Michelle Benato
Lindsay Bennett
Roberta Bennett
Elizabeth Bentley
Kate Benton
Michelle Beresford
Julie Berry
Karen Best
Louise Bevan
Rory Bhandari
Miss Henna Bhatti
Alicia Bills
Kezia Black
Virginia Blackman
Sophie Blake
Karen Blick
Frank Boland

Juliet Bondzio
Karen Booker
Elissa Boreham
Sharon Boultwood
Lucy Bower
Lindsey Bowers
Mark Bowsher
Jason Boyden
Julia Bradbury
Caroline Braithwaite
Perry Braithwaite
Julia Bramble
Nicky Branagh-
   Schmidt
Rachel Bray
Katy Brent
Karen Bretherton
Anna-Maria Bromley
Jason Brown
Claire Brownrigg
Lyndsey Bryce
Andrew Buckingham
Frances Buckley

Phil Buckley
Lucy Buglass
Andrea Burden
Anne Burgot
Jane Burns
Zoe Butcher
Molly Cain
Joseph Calamia
Stephen Calcutt
Laura Calder
Jonny Campbell
Nicholas Campiz
Andy Carpenter
Raechel Carroll
Simon Carwithen
Nicky Chance-
  Thompson
Evie Chrysostomou
Ben Clarke
Louise Clarke
Jules Cliff
Vanessa Cobb
Rose Coburn
Liz Cokayne-Delves
Matt Cole
Scott Coleman
Claire Coles
Alan Coll-Peacock
Alison Collard
Hayley Colley
Louise Collins
Christine Collinson
Emma Compton
Joanna Cook
Tara Cooke
Tina-Marie Cooney
Carol Cooper
Catherine Costigan
Helen Cottage
Sarah Coulthard-
  Evans
Audrey Cowie
Sandra Cox

Brendan Coyle
Sonia Crandall
Sam Crawford
Kenneth Cukier
Heidi Curry
Kate Cushing
Claire Dadds
Jim Daly
Clare Daniels
Julia Davey
Maria David
Claire Davies
Karen Davies
Sylvia Davies
Phil Davies-Pye
Shelley Davis
Su Davis
Adrienne Davitt
Christopher Dawson
Wayne de Leeuw
Alex Denyer
Joanne Derrick
Janet Dewing
Sian Dhillon
Bhanu Dhir
Louise Dhondoo
Carla Di Mambro
Kevin Diamond
Jane Dickinson
Mike Dicks
Michelle Dillon
Sharon Dinsdale
Steve Dobb
Julie Dodds
Emma Dolan
@dollidaydreamer
Sarah Dombrick
Fiona Donaldson
Iain Dootson
Linda Doppenberg-
  van Asperen
Martin Drapper
Charlotte Drury

Kirsty Dunn
Michelle Dunning
Chantelle Dusette
Jane Dyson
Lyn Edmonds
Beatie Edney
Heiko Egeler
Lisa Eléhn
Lisa Ellison
Debbie Else
Lisa English
Verna Esposito
Angie Eustice
Susan Fairley
Maria Felicetti
Gillian Fenner
Cornish Darren
  Fewins
Sandi Fisher
Jen FitzHugh
Daniel Flannigan
Florian Fleitmann
Zoe Flight
Brid Flood
Karin Florencio
Yvonne Foran
Graham Forrest
Jill Fowke
Ellie Freeman
Thomasin Freeman
Anna Friend
Vicki Frost
Joanne Fryett
Julie Fulea
Angela Gajamugan
Sarah Gallacher
Linda Galloway
Olivia Galun
Nicola Galvin
Gaynor Gardner
Melanie Gardner
Sarah Geddis
Milly Gilbert

Samantha Giles
Fiona Gill
Richard Gillin
Richard Gillin
Michael Gilmore
Catherine Glover
Helen Glover
John Goddard
Maria Goddard
Simon Goldsmith
Maria Goodacre
Suzanne Goss
Damon Gough
Gemma Gould
Sam Gray
Danielle Green
Duncan Green
Sophie Green
Tara Green
Anna Gregory
Jacinta Gregory
Laura Grimshaw
Teresa Grubman
Katy Guest
Di Gunn
Bobbie Hall
Edward Hall
M Hall
Debora Halstead
Joanna Hammond
Jan Hares
Tina Harman
Sandra Harper
Sian Harries
Colleen Harris
Louise Harris
Sarah Harris
Michelle Hart
Pennie Haslehurst
Jacinta Hastings
Janis Haw
Danielle Hayes
Kate Hayes

Elleshia Haynes
Julie Heinz
Rachelle Hembury
Mary Hemsworth
Julie Herbert
Gail Hewitt
Susie Hills
Sally Hilton
Richelle Hirst
Natasha Hobday
Diana Hollins
Emma Hollywood
Amanda Holt
Sheena Hope
Kevin Howell
Elizabeth Hudson
Liz Hudston
Stu Huggins
Philip Hughes
Mia Hughes-Smith
Gill Humphreys
Susan Hutchinson
David Hyatt
Scott Ingram
Natalie Irvin
Rosy James
Julie Jarrett
Elaine Jenkins
Amy Jensen
Anna Jewes
Anna Jewes
Caroline Johns
Emily Johnson
Gillian Johnson
Denise Johnston
Gillian Jones
Gwenno Jones
Liz Jones
Margaret Jones
Mysti Jones
Nicola Jones
Keith Jones (dizzy)
Sarah Jordan

Kate & George
Manya Kay
Paula Keane
Emily Keating
Katherine Keen
Andrew Kemp
Hilary Kemp
Rebecca Keyland
Dan Kieran
Jane Kindlen
Penelope Kirkham
Mary Kissinger
Mandy Kloppers
Peter Knipp
Tracy Kusik
Sophia Kyriacou
Yvonne Laird
Laura Lambert
Roberta Lang
Becky Laughton
Stephen Leatherdale
Vicky Lee
Emma Leigh
Kay Leigh
Jacqueline Leonard
Jennifer Lewis
Elaine Li-Koo
Ann Liebeck
Chris Limb
Travis Littlechilds
Nikki Lofting
Yvette logue
Amanda Lorean
Rosalia Louçano
Alex Lovell
Cathy Lowe
Denise Lowe
Sharon Luca
Amelia Lutkus-
   Phillips
Jill MacDonald
Nicky MacEwan
Lavaniya Mahendra

Katy Makepeace-
   Warne
Catherine Makin
Alexandra Manning
Laura Mansell
Anthea Marriott
Louise Martin
Terry Martin
Chris Mason
Jacqueline Mason
Vicky Mather
David Matkins
Rob Matthews
Kim Mauger
Anita Mayren
Erin McCarthy
John McCormack
Lorna McCourt
Denise McDermott
Martin McDonald
Bernadette McEleney
Johanna McGuigan
Iona McKay
Rebecca McKernan
Neil McLaren
Lucy McMahon
Lynda McMahon
Zitah McMillan-
   Ward
Aidan McQuade
Scott McRobert
Sam McTeare
Geoffrey Meenan
Clara Melchor
   Bowman
Lynne Mellor
Emma Menhinnitt
Kimberley Miles
Louise Miles-
   Pascoe
Niall Miller
David Minahan
Mita Mistry

Erika Mitchell
John Mitchinson
Gerard Moore
Michaela Moore
Magda Moorey
Justin Moors
Alasdair Morton
Ysanne Morton
Shola Mos-
   Shogbamimuu
Lisa Moscynski
Simon Mosd
Kate Mosse
Bernard Moxham
Matthew Mudford
Robin Mulvihill
Julie Muncey
Fiona Murden
Ann Murphy
Eamonn Murphy
Siobhan Murphy
Robyn Murray
Lisa Francesca Nand
Nina Nannar
Carlo Navato
Anne Neal
Mark Neeson
Ed Nell
Alison Newnham
Lesley Newton
Debra Ngcobo
Gillian Nicholls
Michelle Nicholls
Lidia Noronha
Nic Northage
Onneke Northcote-
   Green
Christopher Norton
Rob Nunn
Sarah O Reilly
Thomas O
   Shaughnessy
Juliana Orrick

Amanda Osborne
Jessan Dunn Otis
Margaret Oxley
Michael Paley
Giles Paley-Phillips
Alison Palmer
Emma Palmer
Vivien Parry
William James Parry
Sylvia Parsonage
Bev Parsons
Mark Pawsey
Natasha Peach
Esme Pears
Holly Pecyna
Janet Pepsin
Dayna Pereira
Imogen Perrin
Georgina Petty
Charlotte Phillips
Katharine Phillips
Lily Pinhorne
Sarah Pitman
Darrel Poletyllo
Justin Pollard
Vaishali Pratap
Justin Presser
Amber Preston
Beth Procter
Rosemary Purr
Cindy Puzak
Mel Quinn
Nichola Quinn
Rajinder Rai
Susan Randall
JP Rangaswami
Evelyn Rapp
Kaya Rehmani
Quin Rey
Ria
Cheryl Rickman
Thomas Henry
   Cobden Ridgway

Esther Rigby
Pamela Ritchie
Annie Robb
Kate Robison
Karen Roderick
Caroline Ronsley
Dawn Rooney
Nazaneen Rose
Roshanak
Debra Ross
Mechelle Rowe
Penni Rubens
Ruks
Dominic Rust
Barrie Sadler
Jules Saich
Mark Sanders
Sarah Say
John Schneider
Laura Sclanders
Fiona Scott
Russell Scott
Stewart Scott
Donna Sculy
Jenny Seagrove
Manon Sel
Jayne Sharp
David Shattock
Andrew Shaw
Tracey Sherman
Rochelle Shinn
Linda Shoare
Andrea Shore
David Shortt
Amy Sibley-Allen
Sarah Siddall
Lorna Simes
Alison Smith
Diana Smith
Linda Smith
Naomi Smith
Deborah Sockett
Nadia Sohawon

Gemma Southerden
Mary Spelman
Cheryl Stacey
Chris Staunton
Peter Stefanovic
Gillian Stern
Brie Stevens-Hoare
Belinda Steward
Charlotte Stockman
Paul Stokes
David Strauss
Em Stryker
Isy Suttie
Aimee Swayne
Lauraine Sweeney
Jon Swift
Caroline Taylor
Debbie Taylor
Isobel Taylor
Jill Taylor
Joel Taylor
Khloë Terae
Mary Terlizzi
The Lions Barber
   Collective
Carol Theakston
Danny Thomas
Pen Thompson
Sian Thompson
Diane Thomson
Jo-Ann Thorn
Mel Tiley
Joanna Tindall
Annemarie Tissen
Joanna Todd
Polly Todd
Jason Torgerson
Simon Trigwell
Martin Trotter
Nicola Tudge
Kate Tudor
Steve Turner
Tom Tyson

Hilje van Beijnum
Natalie Van
   Blaaderen
Lana Van Thoor
Adam Veenstra
Mark Vent
Victoria Clare Louise
   @v23474
Rebecca Villar
Emma Virgilio
Sharran Wainwright
Christine Walker
Martin Walker
TJ Walker
Steven Walley
Patrick Walsh
Chris Ward
Jackie Ward
Simon Ward
Jennie Wassall-
   Jamieson
Cathy Wassell
Joanna Waterfall
Marc Watson
Miranda Watson
Elen Webb
Mark Webb
Saga Wedin
Julie Weeks
Jenni Welch
Melanie Werner
Julie White
Sharon White
Charlotte Whiteside
Naomi Wilkinson
Chris Williams
Dr Sian Williams
Fraser Williams
Rebecca Williams
Steven Wills
Susan Wilson
Jenn Winchester
Rob Witts

Pauline Woods
Richard Woods
Sonja Woods
Doreen Wright

Justin Wright
Lea Yerevanian
Wing Yeung
Marianne Young

Miss Angela Young
Naomi Young
Lin Zi

With special thanks to the following people for their generous
and 'collectably social' support of this book.

Deborah Bowie – Deborah_Bowie
Nicola Buckland – @nicclesb
Katy Burrows – @KatyJBurrows
Rita Carta Manias
Nick Childs – @nickchilds
Jason Coleman
Shar Cymru
Jon Dyer – @Jon_D_MCMLXXI
Victoria Dyson – @dyson4tea
Ricardo Flores – @EngelAnael
Demi Geraghty – @demideeofficial
Kimberly Gold – @kim_gold77
Lindsey Armet Greenan – @lindseygreenan
Kristin Greenfield
Fernando Gros – @fernandogros
Chris Hartness – @maudiebird25
Lucy Hawkins – @lucyjrhawkins
Joanna Hughes – @johughes27
Kaye Inglis
Vix Leyton – @prvix
Murray Lynes
John Monks
Adam Murphy – @Anonymous_Riter
Phil Phipps – @PhiltheFlipper
Joe Plumb – @JoePlumbUK
Jane Roberts – @JaneRobertsOU
Clair Stewart – @TwystedRoots
Sara Swift-Stafford
Vanessa Viner – @latersbabyuk
Zohrah Zancudi – @zohrah